ALASKAN ABDUCTION TARGET

MEGAN SHORT

If you purchased this book without a cover you should be aware that this book is stolen property. It was reported as "unsold and destroyed" to the publisher, and neither the author nor the publisher has received any payment for this "stripped book."

Recycling programs for this product may not exist in your area.

ISBN-13: 978-1-335-95780-1

Alaskan Abduction Target

For questions and comments about the quality of this book, please contact us at CustomerService@Harlequin.com.

Love Inspired
22 Adelaide St. West, 41st Floor
Toronto, Ontario M5H 4E3, Canada
www.LoveInspired.com

HarperCollins Publishers
Macken House, 39/40 Mayor Street Upper,
Dublin 1, D01 C9W8, Ireland
www.HarperCollins.com

Printed in Lithuania

Jock leaned forward, when *Bang!* A rifle round smashed through the window, narrowly avoiding his head.

Jock grabbed Phoebe's shoulder, shoving her down below the window. Another round fired, hitting the doorframe. Phoebe's heart raced, and she peered over the dash. They'd been lured into a trap!

"Stay down," Jock said, backing the vehicle up.

A man came running toward them, sliding to a rest next to Phoebe's door. "Let me in!"

Phoebe gasped, shrinking back toward Jock, who kept his weapon and eyes trained on the man.

Her hands quivered with adrenaline as she took in the sunken eyes. This was the man who'd tried to kill her. Who'd snatched Charlie! "Jock..."

Another rifle round rang out, slamming into Jock's seat. He flung open the back door. "Get in!"

The man awkwardly slid into the back seat. He shivered, his face red from the cold. How long had he been out there? And why?

Jock took out some cable ties and fastened his handcuffs and the man to the vehicle. "Who's shooting at us?"

The man didn't respond.

Another round fired, this time missing Phoebe by an inch. "We need to go!"

Megan Short is an Australian author of inspirational romantic suspense novels. She grew up in New Zealand, where her favorite activity was watching bumblebees and daydreaming. A screenwriter by trade, she has writing qualifications from UCLA and has won some screenwriting awards. Megan currently lives in Melbourne and loves learning new skills and meeting new people, many of whom make their way into her stories! She still spends too much time daydreaming and is a recovering chocoholic.

Books by Megan Short

Love Inspired Suspense

Alaskan Police Protector
Trapped on the Alaskan Glacier
Alaskan Abduction Target

Visit the Author Profile page at LoveInspired.com.

What man of you, having an hundred sheep,
if he lose one of them, doth not leave the
ninety and nine in the wilderness, and go after
that which is lost, until he find it? And when he
hath found it, he layeth it on his shoulders, rejoicing.
And when he cometh home, he calleth together
his friends and neighbours, saying unto them,
Rejoice with me; for I have found my sheep
which was lost.

—*Luke* 15:4–6

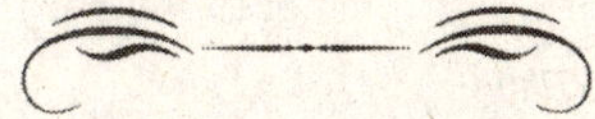

Soli Deo gloria

ONE

"Charlie, come on. I need your help here, bud." Phoebe Tait grasped the hand of her two-year-old son, juggling her oversize luggage with her other hand. *I wish Ronnie was here.* While her late husband, Ronnie, hadn't been much of a help when it came to caring duties, he'd have at least offered a hand. She tried to wrestle the little boy into the stroller.

"No!" Charlie screeched, wriggled and strained, exhausted after more than a day of travel to Cordova, Alaska, from their hometown, Tucson, Arizona. It had taken longer than expected for the luggage to arrive. The announcement had promised a twenty-minute wait when they landed, and most of the other passengers had left with their bags already. It'd been the stroller, of course. *Maybe I shouldn't have bothered.* Having just taken a flying tour over the snow-covered town before landing, she'd come to realize the contraption was probably a little futile here. But she hadn't thought too hard about it when packing, figuring it might come in handy. If the toddler would cooperate, now could be one of those times.

"Come on, Charlie. *Please.*" Phoebe gritted her teeth, hoping the little boy wouldn't hurl himself to the ground and scream like he had during their stopover in Anchorage.

Her cheeks burned with remembered embarrassment. "I'll give you a lollipop if you get in the stroller." She sweetened her tone, hoping the incentive would help. She was just about out of ideas. They'd done all of his busy activities on the plane. His well-loved light brown toy bunny, Mr. Snuffles, had occupied him for a few minutes. The mural on the wall of the airport, with its colorful fireweed, trumpeter swans and schools of fish had captivated Charlie for about ten minutes. But the rest of the time she'd been attempting to stop him from running back toward the tarmac. *What kind of airport doesn't have an air bridge?* At least now that they had the useless stroller, they could go.

Charlie frowned, his little chin jutting out. "No!"

Phoebe closed her eyes, taking a deep breath. *This won't last forever.* It'd been her mantra since Ronnie had died. No, been killed. She had to correct herself. Get out of the mindset that his death had been a terrible accident. The original police investigation had concluded Ronnie drowned. But that didn't explain the strange messages and threats she'd subsequently found on his phone. That had been enough to rouse her suspicions. Then the peculiar break-in at her house confirmed she needed to dig deeper. If Ronnie's death was linked to those events, then his death wasn't an accident. It must have been murder. Well, at least, murder was *probable.* If she didn't believe it, the police wouldn't either. That was why she and Charlie had traveled so far in the winter to this regional fishing village. To convince the police to reopen the case. Calling hadn't worked. The officer in charge of the case had fobbed her off. But he couldn't fob off someone standing in his front office, could he? If only she could convince the police to investigate the new evidence, they'd surely find some answers. She let out a deep, calming breath, opening her eyes. They'd be at the inn soon. She just had to make it to the rental car and strap Charlie into his car seat. She'd done *that* a million times. Then they could have an early night and be at the police station first thing tomorrow. "Okay then, no lollipop for you. We'll walk."

Charlie didn't seem to register what he'd missed out on, confirming Phoebe's guess that the little boy was so tired he didn't know what was going on. If he didn't drop off to sleep while they drove she'd be astonished. At least she could rely on him staying asleep while she transferred him into the portable cot promised by the inn.

Thankfully, the regional airport was tiny, so the walk would be short. The last passengers with oversize luggage hurried toward the doors, skirting around Phoebe.

She wrenched their suitcase into the stroller, using it as a cart to maneuver them toward the exit. Charlie tugged on her arm, and she grimaced as he overextended her shoulder. The old dance injury never quite went away, and Charlie sure didn't help.

"Charlie, could you please slow down? Or would you like a carry?" Phoebe gave his hand a gentle squeeze.

Charlie ignored her, pulling on her arm a little more. They reached the doors, stepping through into the fresh snow blanketing the vicinity. An icy breeze buffeted Phoebe like a slap in the face, and she gave an involuntary gasp. Had Ronnie really worked in these conditions? Sure, he hadn't been here in February, but still… Her gaze raked across the horizon. Snow crusted the mountain range, which stretched toward the sky with an army of spruce trees in the foreground. Under different circumstances, she'd probably consider it beautiful. But today, the freezing environment seemed hostile and foreboding. She checked around for the rental cars, a little envious of the people who were being picked up by friends and relatives. A police vehicle cruised slowly by, crossing paths with a taxi. Maybe she should've ordered a cab too. Driving in these conditions…

Charlie yanked out of her grasp and raced toward a pile of snow, Mr. Snuffles clutched under his arm.

"Charlie!" Phoebe pushed the stroller toward him, rolling her shoulder to try and stop the muscles from stiffening. "Don't just run off!" She stood next to him while he stomped in the snow, his cheeks red from the cold. Thankfully, he was wearing boots. *Now, where's my reservation?* She pulled her phone from her pocket, glad she'd downloaded the paperwork. Who knew what kind of coverage there might be out here in the middle of nowhere.

"You need some help?" A man in a heavy coat, snow boots and a knitted wool hat approached her, carrying a clipboard.

"Yes, please. I booked a rental car. Do you know where I need to go to collect it?" Phoebe felt a little rude keeping her eyes on Charlie most of the time, but it couldn't be helped.

The man gave a little grunt. "No problem. First time here?"

"Yes, it is." Phoebe gave the man the details of her reservation while continuing to eye Charlie, ready to grab him if he made a break for it. For now, the snow pile occupied him. He muttered to Mr. Snuffles in his toddler dialect.

"Unusual time to visit, but there are plenty of winter activities." The man beckoned. "Come follow me. I can grab that case if you'd like."

Phoebe smiled. "Thank you, that'd be great."

"Excuse me." A couple approached the man. "You the guy to talk to about rentals?"

The man nodded. "Sure am. Give me a moment to help this lady, and I'll be right with you."

The couple didn't want to wait, and the man became occupied talking them down.

While he sorted that out, Phoebe wrangled the suitcase by herself. Placing it on the sidewalk for the man, she took the opportunity to pack down the stroller. She'd sling that over her good shoulder. A gray truck pulled up nearby, and a man climbed out, leaving the engine running. Something about him seemed familiar. Phoebe licked her lips, turning to Charlie. "Come on, buddy, we're going to find our car."

"Okay, ma'am, this way." The man with the clipboard grabbed her suitcase, which got caught on the stroller strap. "Oh, hold on."

Phoebe untangled the strap and allowed the man to take her suitcase. She turned to Charlie. The little boy was gone, his bunny left behind in the snow pile. Phoebe's stomach plunged.

"Charlie!" Phoebe dropped the stroller pack to the ground, whirling around to look for her son. She grabbed Mr. Snuffles off the ground, tucking him under her arm. Her son wouldn't leave his bunny. Where had he gone? The door to the gray truck slammed shut, and Phoebe's gut curdled. Suddenly, she remembered exactly from where she recognized that man. Stocky, slightly sunken eyes, around six feet. He'd been waiting outside her house a few weeks ago. He'd been wearing clothes appropriate to Tucson then, not the heavy snow gear he had on just now, which explained why it didn't click right away. *Charlie!*

She raced toward the vehicle, but before she could get close it accelerated toward the highway. "No! Charlie!" No way she could catch it on foot. Her heart raced, and she reached for the man with the clipboard, who'd paused with her suitcase, a confused expression on his face. "He took my son! The police! They were just here!"

"Hold on, slow down. You're saying the police took your son? Really?" The man frowned.

"There's no time to explain!" She had to get the police. They'd help her find that gray truck. Phoebe ran in the direction the police vehicle had gone earlier, slipping and sliding on the sidewalk. There it sat, parked. Empty. *Where are they?* Phoebe resisted the urge to scream in frustration. The airport wasn't big, so they couldn't be far.

She turned, ran back into the bright blue terminal building and ploughed straight into the solid frame of a police officer.

He grabbed her arms before she could bounce off him. "Whoa, easy there."

Phoebe let out a slight sob. "My son! He's been taken!"

The officer had kind hazel eyes, and his brow furrowed. "Just now?" He reached for his radio. "What did you see?"

Phoebe described what had happened as quickly as she could. Thankfully, the officer walked at a brisk pace with her to the door as they talked, then called in the description on his radio.

"Okay, let's go." He raced toward the police vehicle, gesturing for Phoebe to ride shotgun. Flipping on the lights and sirens, he pulled out of the parking lot and accelerated after the truck. "Don't worry, we'll find him." Something about his tone reassured her.

"Thank you, Officer." Phoebe gripped the seat, straining to see if the truck was in view.

"I'm Officer Jock O'Halloran. Call me Jock." He gunned the engine, pulling around a vehicle and passing another.

"I'm Phoebe Tait. My son's name is Charlie." Her voice cracked a little as she said his name. "He's all I have."

What does that man want with Charlie?

* * *

Officer Jock O'Halloran had been conducting a routine security check at the Merle K. Mudhole Smith Airport when Phoebe had accosted him about her son. The woman was petite, with dark hair cascading down her back in soft waves. Her deep brown, almond-shaped eyes had smudges of fatigue under them, and she had a strength and a vulnerability about her that made Jock pay attention. Well, that and her body slamming him. The woman held a well-loved toy bunny, which she absent-mindedly fondled like a security blanket. Must be her son's. Jock's heart contracted. He had a soft spot for children and animals and longed for a houseful of both. *Maybe one day, Lord willing.*

"That's the truck!" Phoebe leaned forward, pointing toward a gray F-150. The vehicle was a dot in the distance. The woman must have great eyesight. Jock estimated there'd been about four inches of fresh snow this morning, and while the plow had been through, the roads were getting a little drifty. He'd put the police vehicle into four-wheel, so it'd normally be okay. But he had a bit of distance to cover if he was to catch up with that truck.

"Hold on tight."

Jock had seen his fair share of cars spinning out on slippery roads, and the thought of an unrestrained toddler in a car wreck chilled his blood. No way he'd let that happen now. *Where's he going?* The small coastal town of Cordova, Alaska, where Jock had lived his whole life, was located at the mouth of the Copper River, right on Prince William Sound. Surrounded by the Chugach National Forest, vast mountain peaks and the sea, the only way out was by boat or plane.

"Do you know this individual?" Jock had gotten bare bones from Phoebe's initial description. Enough to put out a BOLO, but he'd figured they could talk more while they chased him.

"No. I think I've seen him before, back home. But I don't know what he wants with Charlie." Her voice cracked. "He's just a little boy." She held the bunny to her chest.

"Where's home?"

"Tucson, Arizona." Phoebe clutched the bunny to her mouth. "I can't believe this is happening."

He needed to get her to focus. She might be able to shed some light on this individual, maybe give him an idea of the motive. "Why did you come to Cordova?"

Phoebe sighed. "We can worry about that later. Let's concentrate on Charlie."

What a strange thing to say. If it were just *visiting relatives* or *sightseeing*, she could've said. Must be something else. Maybe a custody battle? That was one reason he'd been cautious about getting into a relationship. There was so much at stake. Especially for any children. His mom had proved that.

"Do you think Charlie's father is involved?"

Phoebe let out a frustrated sound. "He's dead."

Jock's heart sank. "I'm sorry."

She didn't bother to respond, and Jock didn't blame her. Phoebe was right about one thing. If the boy's father was dead, it wasn't about custody.

The taillights on the truck lit up, and it slowed. Jock gained on him.

"Is he stopping?" Phoebe voiced his thoughts.

"Let's see. Whatever happens, you need to stay in the vehicle. He may be armed."

She sobbed. "Oh no."

"I will do everything in my power to get your son back safely. I promise." Jock had been careful not to promise to get her son back safely. There were no guarantees. *Lord, please protect this innocent child.*

The vehicle stopped, the door flew open and a man leaned out, dumping a bundle on the roadside.

"Charlie!" Phoebe screamed.

The door slammed and the truck peeled off, headed toward town. Jock's nostrils flared. What sort of person dumped a child on the side of the road?

Jock grabbed his radio, updating the dispatcher to send paramedics as he pulled up to where the child had been left. He leaped from the car, leaving the lights and sirens on to alert passing traffic. "Stay there!"

Too late. Phoebe had already thrown open the door and was right behind him. Jock admired her for it. No mom worth her salt would be parted from her child in need. A wailing cry came from behind a snow berm. *Thank You, Lord.* A cry meant the child was alive. Jock scrambled over the berm and grabbed the boy.

Charlie flailed around, obviously unsure whether Jock was someone he could trust. "Mama! Mamaaa!"

"Hi, Charlie. It's okay. Your mom's right here." Jock soothed him.

"Charlie." Phoebe tugged on Jock's arm, pulling the child toward her. "Oh, sweet boy, Mommy's here." She clutched the toddler to her, and the child wailed, nuzzling into her neck.

"Let's get him into the warmth." Jock helped Phoebe into the back seat with the child, whose cries had calmed to sobbing hiccups. Phoebe thrust the toy bunny into Charlie's hands, which comforted him more.

Jock radioed dispatch to update them, then leaned in. "May I check him for injuries, please? I'm a trained paramedic." Jock had started his career with the fire department as a paramedic, mostly to appease his mom. But he'd gravitated toward law enforcement—the career that had ended his father's life when Jock was around Charlie's age. How different his life would've been if his father had lived.

"Sure, thanks." Phoebe shuffled over to let him sit in the back with them.

Jock carefully peeled back the rough blanket that the kidnapper had wrapped him in. "Hey there, buddy. I'm going to check if you're okay." He smiled, then gently stroked the boy's hair off his forehead and began his examination.

The little boy rubbed his eyes, seemingly unbothered by Jock poking and squeezing his little body. He'd probably have a few bruises, but nothing seemed to be broken.

"He seems okay. The paramedics will take him to the medical center when they get here." Jock climbed out of the vehicle and surveyed the scene. The truck was long gone, now. Why take Charlie just to dump him minutes later? Maybe the kidnapper had panicked when he saw the police pursuit. He could've guessed that the police would have to stop for the child, allowing him to get away. That calculation had been correct. No way Jock would leave the child to go after that truck. He sighed. Thankfully, he'd gotten close enough to give the plate number to dispatch. While the truck might be a popular make and model, there were only so many places to hide here. He sure wouldn't be boarding the ferry undetected.

The paramedics arrived quickly, and within ten minutes had checked Charlie and agreed with Jock's assessment. The boy had been well wrapped, and the soft powder had kept him from harm. Even so, they'd take him to get checked out by a pediatrician.

Phoebe's relief tugged at Jock's heartstrings, reminding him of his own widowed mom. *Lord, please protect*

Phoebe and her son. They have a long road ahead of them. Please walk with them.

"You go with him, and I'll follow." Jock helped Phoebe into the back of the ambulance and shut the door behind the paramedic. He reached for his radio. "Any update on that truck?"

"Not yet, O'Halloran. I have Garrison and Miller out on patrol," the dispatcher replied. Jock sucked his teeth. They'd find it eventually. He'd make sure of that.

"Copy that. I'm headed to the medical center now." Jock climbed back into the cruiser and pulled out onto the highway. Snowflakes pattered against his windshield. Would the snow slow the kidnapper down? Jock had no doubt the man would try to take Charlie again. Phoebe and Charlie remained in danger until he was caught.

Thirty minutes later, Phoebe and Charlie walked into the waiting room where Jock sat. She seemed surprised to see him. Phoebe held the toddler, his head nestled on her shoulder, his bunny gripped in one hand.

"How's Charlie?" Jock rose, moving toward them.

"Tired, but physically fine." She gave him a small smile. "I'm grateful you were there. If you hadn't acted so quickly, I hate to think what would've happened." She frowned. "Why do you think he let Charlie go?"

Jock shrugged. "We won't know until we catch him, but my guess is he panicked when he saw the lights and sirens. It happens."

Phoebe shook her head. "Whatever the reason, I'm glad."

"We need to catch him before he tries again. You mentioned you might've seen the man before?" He gestured for her to sit. The waiting room was mostly empty, so no one would overhear their conversation.

She paled, sitting. "Yes. Like I said, he'd been outside my house."

"Any thoughts as to why?"

"Maybe." She sighed. "I was planning to come to the police station tomorrow. It's a long conversation." The smudges of tiredness under her eyes had deepened. The poor woman must be exhausted. Charlie had already closed his eyes and was softly snuffling on his mom's shoulder.

"Look, I can see how tired you both are. How about you give me a few details now, and I'll get you to your accommodation. I can follow up on what you tell me and go over everything in detail tomorrow." He reached into his pocket and pulled out a bag of jellybeans. "Here, have some of these. It'll help."

Phoebe held out her palm, and Jock poured a few of the sweets out for her. "Thanks." She chewed one, thinking. "Well, as I mentioned, my husband is dead. He died here in Cordova. Well, offshore, to be precise. Your department investigated the death, but the case is closed. Accidental death. But it wasn't an accident."

Jock leaned forward, blinking. "What makes you think that?"

"I had some suspicions about what he'd been doing because I couldn't access his messages. The court recently approved my request to have the phone company give me access. What I found shocked me. I have everything in my suitcase. All the hard copies. Also, I've saved them on the cloud."

"Can you give me some idea of what they said?"

Phoebe glanced around her, as if concerned about being overheard. "The week before he died, there was a message saying something along the lines of if he didn't cooperate, there'd be trouble. There were others leading up to it. But isn't it a coincidence that he's being threatened, and then days later he's dead?"

Jock's eyebrows drew together. "I can see your point. What does this have to do with the kidnapper?"

She held her son a little closer. "He was outside my house the week after the court order came through. Don't you find that suspicious? Like maybe I've uncovered something they don't want me to find?" She shoved the rest of the jellybeans into her mouth, anxiously munching on them.

"Did you call the police in Tucson?" Jock's muscles tightened.

"No, it was just a suspicion. What were they going to do?" She cradled Charlie to her, stroking his dark brown hair. "I guess I should have. I wish I had."

"Okay, we can talk about that later. I called the airport, and Joe has your suitcase. You're staying at the inn, right?"

"Yes." She accepted his hand to help her up.

"Let's get you settled in there, then in the morning I'll come pick you up."

They walked through the doors toward the police vehicle, Jock holding his hand over Charlie's face to shield him from the snow. A few yards from the vehicle, bright lights flicked on, an engine revved and the gray F-150 accelerated toward them. A sudden feeling of cold flooded Jock's chest. He'd underestimated the kidnapper. *Lord, help me do better.*

TWO

Phoebe froze when headlights illuminated the driveway, blinding her. She clutched Charlie tight, her mouth hanging open as the dark gray pickup sped toward them. Before she could move, Jock's arms wrapped around her and Charlie, yanking them out of harm's way.

The engine sound deafened her, and the slipstream of the truck whipped past far too closely. So close the truck's mirror banged against the officer's shoulder, snapping back with a loud click. Jock grunted. Hopefully he wasn't too badly injured. Snow from the vehicle spattered her and Charlie, and she pulled her son in tighter. He grumbled and fussed in his sleep, snuggling Mr. Snuffles into his chest.

Jock propelled them back inside, one hand on his radio, the other massaging his shoulder. "All units, officer in need of assistance." He rattled off the details of the medical center and the truck's plates, then turned to them. "Are you hurt?" Concern creased his brow.

A nurse raced toward them. "I saw that truck! Are you injured?" She reached for Jock's shoulder.

"I'm sure it's just a bruise." Jock held up his hand with a wince.

Somehow, Charlie remained asleep, and Phoebe slid into the chair she'd occupied moments earlier. The attacker meant business. She stroked Charlie's head, shaking a little from the adrenaline. What if Jock hadn't stayed with them? Phoebe kissed Charlie's head, thankful the officer had been there.

She thought of the threatening messages she'd discovered on her husband's messaging account and shivered. The sooner Jock had those in his possession, the better. At least he hadn't dismissed her concerns out of hand. She'd expected a little resistance from the police. After all, they had closed the file. But they couldn't ignore what had happened now.

Having satisfied the nurse that he didn't need medical attention, Jock crouched next to Phoebe.

"Thanks for saving Charlie—us—again." Phoebe rubbed her hand down her son's back.

Jock leaned against the armrest. "Are you okay?"

"I'm fine, thanks. Do you think it's safe for us to stay at the inn? If he could find us here, he can find us there." She shuddered.

His brow creased. "I agree. While my mom's friend Caroline runs the inn—and she's ex-navy—it's too hard to defend. All the rooms are accessible from the street."

Phoebe's stomach flipped. The thought of someone climbing through the window and grabbing Charlie… "Where will I stay?"

"My mom's house." Jock cleared his throat.

Phoebe frowned. "That's a lot to ask. I'm not sure—"

"Mom won't mind at all. She has a couple of spare rooms, so I can take one, and you can take the other. That way we can keep you safe, and I can stay by your side until we catch this guy." Jock's tone sounded friendly, but an undertone suggested he'd made up his mind. He gave her a reassuring smile. “Cordova’s small, there aren’t many places to hide. We’ll catch him.”

Phoebe swallowed. “Are you *sure* your mom won’t mind?”

Jock gave her a sympathetic frown. “Trust me, she will love having you. Once you meet her, you’ll understand.”

Phoebe pursed her lips in thought. That seemed too good to be true, and in Phoebe’s experience, that meant there’d be a catch. She’d have to remain vigilant. For her and for Charlie. Jock might seem nice enough, but she didn’t know him. She needed to keep her guard up.

Forty minutes later, Phoebe cuddled Charlie in the back of Jock’s police vehicle, as Jock turned into a quiet residential street. She’d given her statement about the truck incident to Officer Samuel Miller, who’d shown up with his K-9 husky, and another officer whose name she forgot. Charlie had slept through the whole thing.

Jock pulled into the driveway of a modest two-story whitewashed wooden bungalow with front steps leading to a stoop covered with a small portico. Shadows from the streetlights framed the cross-gabled roofline, and each of the teal-framed windows had a welcoming yellow glow behind the curtains. Spruce trees lined the backyard, their snow-sprinkled tops peeking over the roofline, illuminated by the reflected light from the house.

Jock parked in front of the garage and walked around to open Phoebe’s door. Phoebe handed the sleeping Charlie to him, then climbed from the back seat. Before she could make it up the first step, the front door swung open and an older woman with Jock’s eyes and smile came to help her.

“Phoebe, I’m Marge.” She gazed adoringly at Charlie, who’d nestled right into Jock’s arms. “And this must be Charlie. Let’s get you inside out of this snow.”

Phoebe followed Marge up the icy steps, thankful for Jock's help. No use worrying about her pride when carrying Charlie another few yards would be too much for her. It'd be much worse to slip on the steps and drop him.

Jock came behind carrying Charlie and shut the door after them. There'd been no sign of the gray truck, so hopefully the driver had given up for the night. The police escort probably hadn't hurt. She glanced through the front window to see Officer Miller backing down the driveway. Maybe she could relax for now.

Marge's house had to be the definition of cozy. Phoebe followed her down a wood-paneled hall lined with family photos, which led to a living room. Comfortable sofas with granny-square afghans and colorful cushions surrounded a crackling open fire that scented the room with woodsmoke. Sweet and savory smells from the adjacent kitchen wafted toward her, reminding her of how long it'd been since her last meal.

"I'm sure you'd like to wash up, hon, and get Charlie down for the night. Follow Jock to your room and get all settled in. Dinner will be ready soon." The warmth in Marge's voice sent a pang through Phoebe's heart. She tried to remember a time her own mom had spoken to her like that, but came up empty.

"That sounds great, thanks." *So much for keeping your guard up.* Phoebe had never been good at that, which had been her downfall.

Jock had already disappeared into the bedroom, and she followed him in. The room was situated right next to the bathroom. Soft lighting brightened the bedroom, which had been painted pale pink. Slightly darker pink curtains with matching pelmets framed the window, which looked out onto the backyard. A rug in pastel green with pink roses had been laid under the white-painted cast-iron bed frame topped with soft pink sheets, a comforter and pillows. A cot had been set up next to the bed with blue sheets and a warm toddler sleeping bag, and Jock had gently laid Charlie down.

"I'll let you do the rest." He spoke quietly, stepping toward the door.

Phoebe tilted her head toward him. Jock seemed like a bit of an expert. Did he have children of his own? She hadn't seen a ring on his finger. And presumably if he had a family, he wouldn't be staying here with her. No, she had to stop wondering such things. She needed to keep things formal.

She'd give him more on the case—remind them both where they stood. "Hold on, I have something for you before you go."

Jock paused at the door. "Sure."

Phoebe sat on the bed and reached into the diaper bag. She pulled out the notes she'd taken about Ronnie's death. "I should've given you these before. It's notes, and a timeline I made about Ronnie's death."

Jock sat next to her and flipped through her notes. "He was a fisherman?"

"Yes. He worked offshore." She swallowed. "I guess you weren't involved in his case?"

"Sorry, no. This is the first I've heard of it. Tomorrow I'll pull out the file and go through it."

Phoebe's face reddened. She didn't like asking for any favors. But she needed this to end soon. "I hope you'll let me go through it too. I feel like I know the case really well. The other officer I spoke with on the phone—Officer MacNally—didn't seem too interested once he'd decided it was an accidental death."

Jock licked his lips. "I'm sorry about that. MacNally

was transferred to Fairbanks a few weeks ago. I can't just reopen a case. It has to go by the chief."

"Oh." Phoebe's chin tilted down. "Do you think he'll agree?"

"It's not up to me." Jock seemed genuinely concerned. "I'll explain about the attacks, and if I get those messages and have a look at them—"

"Could it be *we*, please? I really want to be involved in this. I know Ronnie and the case better than anyone. Especially now the officer in charge of the file has left." Phoebe blinked rapidly.

"It's not up to me," Jock repeated.

Before Phoebe could press him further, Marge poked her head through the door, giving a soft smile when she noticed Charlie's slumber. "Dinner's ready when you are," she whispered.

Phoebe, Jock and Marge converged on the dining room table, which had been set for four, including a high chair. They wouldn't need it. Charlie was out for the count. A neutral linen tablecloth and matching napkins had been set with handmade pottery plates glazed with teal blue, silver cutlery and crystal glassware. Marge had roasted a chicken, and the aroma of lemon, garlic and thyme made Phoebe's mouth water.

Jock pulled out a chair for Phoebe. "I hope you're not a vegetarian."

Phoebe laughed. "I think even if I were, this'd turn me." She accepted the slices of chicken breast Marge served her, along with crispy roasted potatoes, steamed carrots and greens. "Thanks."

Once they'd all been served, Marge bowed her head. "For this and all we are about to receive, make us truly grateful, Lord. Through Christ, we pray. Amen."

"Amen," Jock and Phoebe repeated. It'd been a while since Phoebe had said a blessing over food. Ronnie had been a Christian in name only, and she hadn't eaten a meal with her mom in years. After Ronnie's death, she'd begun to wonder whether it was God's punishment for her being so lax in her faith. But Marge's faith put her at ease, and in spite of her intentions, she relaxed.

The meal had to be one of the best home-cooked dinners Phoebe had ever tasted. If only she could learn to cook like this one day, she'd be a happy woman. Her own mom had been more of a throw-everything-in-the-pot-and-hope-for-the-best kind of cook, which may be nourishing but not exactly something Phoebe had aspired to. Her own attempts at roasting chicken for Ronnie had been a little on the dry side, no matter how many online tutorials she watched. Ronnie hadn't minded, though, he'd just turf the meal and order takeout for himself.

Phoebe ate her fill and placed her cutlery on her plate. "Thank you for this delicious meal, Marge. I'm so grateful for your kindness. Having me and Charlie here, and…"

Marge reached over and squeezed Phoebe's hand. "You're very welcome. I vividly remember being a young widow, like you, with my husband killed at work. Jock was a toddler, probably the same age as Charlie is now, and I was pregnant with his sister, Wallace, at the time. I'm sure my worries then are similar to yours now. You can stay here as long as you need."

Tears threatened, and Phoebe blinked them away. She wasn't normally this emotional, and she couldn't let it show now. She was here for one purpose only: Ronnie's case. "I didn't realize you lost your husband. I'm so sorry to hear that."

Jock cleared his throat. "Mom, Phoebe's not here for chitchat."

Marge sobered. "I'm sorry, you're right. You need to get some sleep so you can catch whoever's doing this."

A weight filled Phoebe's chest. While she'd like to hear a little more about how Marge managed to raise such a thoughtful and generous son on her own, Jock was right. She was not here for conversation.

Lord, I know we haven't been on speaking terms, but I hope You'll forgive me. I think I need Your help. Whoever was after her and Charlie wasn't going to stop.

Jock didn't sleep well. Staying alert to possible intruders mixed with thoughts of Phoebe and Charlie's predicament kept him perpetually half awake. The familiar noises in the night were interrupted by Charlie waking with a cry, and Phoebe soothing him back to sleep. He resisted the urge to check if they were okay—the woman deserved some privacy. She intrigued him. Why travel to a remote Alaskan town in winter with a toddler? Surely she knew she could be stuck here if the weather turned. He tried to put himself in her position and failed to see how traveling would help. Was she reckless or just desperate? Must be more to this. He tossed and turned, unable to get comfortable in his old bed. The bruised shoulder didn't help. Should he take Phoebe's word for it that the attacks were related to her husband's case? It was possible they were two separate problems. Also possible that Phoebe held something back. Officer Miller, his mentor and friend, would tell him not to jump to conclusions without evidence. But the coincidences didn't sit well with Jock. *I'll assume they're connected until proven otherwise.*

The next day, after his mom had fed them a hearty

cooked breakfast, they made it to the police department without incident. Joe had dropped Phoebe's suitcase off before they'd left, allowing Phoebe to change Charlie and herself into fresh clothes and retrieve her paperwork. Marge had offered for Charlie to stay with her, and given how Charlie had taken to Marge and her big box of "big boy" toys, Phoebe had a hard time protesting. Her main concern was about Charlie being snatched again. In the end, Jock had convinced Phoebe that his mom's house would be safe enough. There'd been no sign of the gray truck, and officers would patrol in that area until they'd caught the guy. Besides, having a toddler at the PD wasn't a good idea.

Jock's shoulder still ached, but he tried to ignore it. He brought out the file from Phoebe's husband's death, but before he could open it, she leaned forward, handing over a manila folder of her own. A waft of her vanilla perfume scented the air. "I'm glad Joe dropped my suitcase off so quickly. Here are the messages from my husband's phone."

Jock set Ronnie's case file aside and opened Phoebe's, flicking through the pages.

She continued. "He never gave me his passwords, so I couldn't access them right away. As I mentioned before, I had to apply to the court to get access to his cloud, which took a while." She rubbed her hands on her legs.

Jock tilted his head to the side, impressed with her tenacity. He skimmed the messages. The general theme was a threat that if Ronnie didn't "get his head straight," there would "be trouble." The sender had used *precede* when they meant *proceed*. Precede with the plan, or else. A common mistake, but he wasn't dealing with an English professor. What was Ronnie supposed to be getting straight in his head? Wasn't detailed in the messages. Had the threat of trouble been fulfilled in his death? The initial messages predated Ronnie's drowning by several weeks. Then the later ones, less than a week.

"Is this all of them?" He met her gaze.

"From this cell phone number, yes." She frowned. "I can still access them, but I printed them just in case something happens to his account."

"Good idea." Although the messages seemed reasonably secure given the hoops Phoebe had to jump through to access them, he appreciated her caution. He closed the folder. "Do you mind if I keep these?"

"I have copies at home too. These are for you." Her hands brushed his when she handed over the files.

He cleared his throat. "Thanks. Is there anything else you want me to look at before I go through your husband's file?"

She shook her head.

"Is this the only reason you think his death wasn't accidental?"

Phoebe gave him a look. "You mean apart from the kidnapping and that guy trying to run us all over?"

Jock frowned. "I mean *before*. Something made you suspicious enough to contact the police station and then travel here."

"Like I said, that man started watching the house." Her shoulders drooped. "There was something about him that didn't sit right. I'd never seen him before, and then I applied to the court for access to Ronnie's cloud and contacted the Cordova PD. Next day, there he was. It seemed like too much of a coincidence. Like he must've been keeping tabs on me, or on Ronnie's file. Why would he do that if an accidental drowning occurred?" She bounced a curled knuckle against her mouth. "Then there was the break-in."

Break-in? He leaned forward, waiting for her to continue.

"Charlie and I were out for the day, and when we came back, someone had broken in. But they didn't take anything. They'd riffled through the study, broken open the filing cabinet and ripped apart the closet." Her voice hitched. "But they'd left my jewelry, other things of value. It was like they were looking for something specific."

Jock's heart rate picked up. "Did you file a police report?"

"Yes, though I didn't connect the man with the break-in at the time." She sighed. "It was a difficult time. Charlie wasn't sleeping, and..."

He gave her a sympathetic smile. She didn't have to say the rest. Grieving the loss of a husband took a toll, as did raising a toddler solo.

"The police were surprised they didn't take anything. They gave me the report for insurance so I could claim for the damage, but didn't seem very interested." She bit her lip. "I mean, they were nice enough."

"But they probably have other crimes to solve." Jock understood. Cordova PD wasn't a busy place. Everything from a missing trash can to a minor traffic accident got investigated. Wouldn't be like that in a big city like Tucson. "I have to ask. Is there anything else going on in your life that might have caused this man to follow you? Did Ronnie have any debts?"

She shook her head.

"Is there anyone who might have waited until Ronnie was out of the picture before trying to get to you? Something from your past?"

"No."

Jock frowned. "What about *your* workplace?"

Phoebe pressed her lips together. "You think I haven't already thought of that? My family is a little dysfunctional, but nothing special. I'm a professional dancer. Well, I was before Charlie came along. I used to dance in a contemporary lyrical troupe, but it's too intense when you have a baby. Now, I teach little kids to dance. I'm not in a high-risk profession for stalkers or killers."

Jock's postured stiffened with surprise. He hadn't met a professional dancer before. Guess that explained her gracefulness.

Her thought process made sense, but he didn't like what *wasn't* in Phoebe's file. Seemed like there'd be more messages giving Ronnie instructions. Unless those had been given verbally. There'd be no accessible record of Ronnie's conversations, especially if he used the same encrypted messaging application to make voice calls. Maybe he'd have to get a subpoena of his own. *If* the chief agreed to reopen the case.

"Okay, let's see what we have here." He opened the file, recognizing the photo he'd pulled up from the electronic file. Ronnie Tait didn't have a kind face, even considering it was a grainy DMV photo. Heat rose in his body, and his protective instinct kicked in. Did that explain Phoebe's behavior? She seemed suspicious of people and surprised when anyone showed her the least bit of human decency. But if the man hadn't been a kind husband, why would she be spending so much time and energy trying to seek justice for him? It was a big imposition given Charlie and teaching would keep her busy enough. Could she be after a wrongful death lawsuit? If there'd been negligence, she might have a case. He needed more information.

He started with the case summary. Ronnie Tait had gone overboard, and despite the best efforts of the crew, resurfaced too late to save. Unfortunately, this wasn't uncommon on smaller offshore boats of the kind Ronnie had been working on. Commercial fishing was rated one of the most hazardous occupations in America for a reason.

Reading through each of the numerous reports with care, he searched for any unusual circumstances surrounding the drowning. The further he went, the more the case appeared to be a textbook accidental death. The detailed reports confirmed Ronnie had been on an offshore fishing vessel in the Bering Sea. He'd been tipped overboard when a large wave appeared unexpectedly and drowned. They attempted to revive him but were unsuccessful. A medical examiner's report concluded that Ronnie had drowned—the plume of froth around the mouth and the increased lung markings on the postmortem CT scan confirmed the police's report. Nothing in the toxicology report suggested he'd been intoxicated. Statements from the crew of the fishing vessel were consistent—possibly a little too consistent, but that was normal if they'd had a chance to talk about the incident before being interviewed. The employer, Cordova Fisheries LLC, had been investigated but found to have followed the standard safety procedures. Nothing suggested foul play or negligence. Every report had been signed correctly; there were no procedural shortcuts. No inconsistencies or laziness.

But with the attempted kidnapping and last night's attack, surely Chief Anderson would agree to further investigation. He'd been the one to sign off on closing the case, and he wouldn't like that the man's widow was under attack. He'd have to make sure he could convince the boss because he wasn't ready to say no to Phoebe. He glanced up from the file, and his pulse picked up. Her face had paled, and she leaned back in the chair.

Jock closed the file and leaned toward her. "Are you feeling okay? Do you need anything?" It was possible the poor woman hadn't slept much, and she'd barely touched her breakfast, more focused on Charlie's needs.

She stretched her arms over her head, wincing. "Maybe some fresh air and something to eat. I'd also like to check in on Charlie."

"That sounds like a good idea. I'll drive, and you can call my mom."

Ten minutes later, Phoebe had satisfied herself that Charlie was completely safe and happy. They'd been seated at the local café and were poring over the menu. The café seemed quiet for a Friday, and they'd been able to sit right near the front where the cold ocean breeze from the harbor trickled in through the slightly open window. Clouds blanketed Orca Inlet and a light dusting of snow persisted.

Jock already knew what he'd order—his usual amber-beer-battered Alaskan halibut with jalapeño tartar sauce and fries. He used the time to study Phoebe, whose eyes roved the menu. The color had returned to her cheeks, and she seemed a little more relaxed. Must be stressful to be investigating her husband's death when she'd initially believed it to be an accident. There was something about her that triggered his protective instincts.

"I can't decide." She gave Jock a doleful glance. "What are you getting?"

Jock pointed to the fish and chips. "The jalapeño is a little spicy, though, so depends if you like spice..."

Phoebe grinned. "I'm a big fan of spice." The grin that lit up her face softened something in Jock's heart that he hadn't felt before. He broke her gaze, thankful for the server's approach.

Nancy was a skinny woman in her thirties whose

bleached-blond ponytail swung as she walked. She came bearing drinks—black coffee for Jock and water for Phoebe.

"Your usual, hon?" Nancy asked Jock, pulling a pad and pen out of her apron pocket.

"Make it two, please." He looked at Phoebe. "Do you want anything else?"

"I'll see how I go with that, thanks." Phoebe's smile had lost the animation of her earlier grin. Like she'd remembered why they were here.

"Won't be long." Nancy walked toward the kitchen.

"I guess you come here a lot?" Phoebe pulled napkins and cutlery from the canister and set some in front of Jock, then herself.

Jock shrugged. "Probably once a week. Bruce usually comes away with some scraps, so it's popular with Miller."

"Bruce?"

"Officer Miller's K-9."

Recognition dawned on Phoebe's face. "The husky. I was surprised they let him in the medical center."

"Yeah, he goes everywhere. He's the best. I hope I'll get a K-9 of my own one day." His stomach tensed. Why did he confide that to Phoebe? He hadn't exactly advertised his desire for a working dog. Besides, the chief would have to sign off on training first.

"I'm sure you'd be good at it. Charlie loves dogs." She smiled.

Jock's heart ached a little. How he longed to be a father. But he had to accept the reality of his lot in life. With his sister moving to Florida with her young son for her husband's three-year deployment with the US Coast Guard, he'd committed to being there for Mom. And in Cordova, there were few available women. *Lord, I accept Your will.*

Even if it hurt. He forced a smile. "Charlie seems like a great kid."

She nodded and gazed out the window, a wistful look in her eye. Maybe thinking about her late husband.

Jock observed a young man enter the café, and his whole body tensed. Dressed in a worn-out winter coat and scruffy boots, Jock didn't recognize him. He must've sensed Jock's eyes on him because he turned around, staring as if trying to focus his gaze, which darted to and fro. Jock had seen it before—the hidden underside of Alaska's drug problem.

Jock turned to Phoebe to reassure her that he'd handle it, but she'd paled, her hands to her mouth.

"I've seen him before," she stuttered. "There was a photo of him in Ronnie's phone. I didn't think anything of it…"

The young man turned his attention to Phoebe, and her breathing picked up. He pulled a knife, stepped toward her, then lunged at her throat.

Not on my watch!

THREE

Adrenaline coursed through Jock's body. He stepped between the young man and Phoebe, grabbed the assailant's arm and shoulder and twisted it until the man yowled, releasing the grip on the knife. It dropped to the ground with a clang, and Phoebe's breath caught.

Jock whipped the assailant onto his stomach and cuffed him, reading him his rights. The few other patrons burst into a round of applause, and Jock prayed that his embarrassment wasn't obvious. He'd been doing his job, nothing more. But before he could say so, a shotgun blast smashed through the front window.

"Get down!" Jock released his grip on the assailant and leaped toward Phoebe.

Phoebe had already hit the floor, eyes wide. She stared at Jock, dots of blood speckling her face.

"Are you hit?" Protectiveness welled within him, and he reached for Phoebe's hand. "You're bleeding."

She touched her face with her free hand. "Just glass from the window. I'm fine." She let him give her hand a squeeze. Another shot fired through the other window, showering the tables in glass. He had to protect the other patrons too.

"Stay down!" Jock checked the other customers, who'd sensibly taken cover. One of the older men had pulled his own Ruger. Jock didn't discourage him; he could do with the backup, and he recognized the man from the gun club.

"I called 911." Nancy's breathless voice called from behind the counter. "Help is on the way." Thankfully, the police department was located close by.

Jock reached for his radio, updating dispatch before crawling toward the front of the diner to get a closer look. His heart raced as he peered over the threshold. Another blast shattered the remaining window, and Jock ducked for cover.

Sirens sounded in the distance, and Jock raised his gun, ready to fire. He grabbed a ketchup bottle and pushed it into the line of fire. When nothing happened, he peeked again. The taillights of the gray truck backed toward him. *He's escaping.* Couldn't let him get away again. Jock leaped to his feet, threw open the door and sprinted toward the truck. The gray truck screeched away, and Jock aimed at the rear window, shooting it out. That didn't slow down the vehicle, and Jock grabbed his radio. "He's headed south, I repeat, south."

Hopefully someone would catch the truck. Sadly, it wouldn't be him. He had to go check on the others and make sure the young man hadn't tried to escape. Was he associated with the guy in the truck? Phoebe had said she recognized him.

He jogged up the steps, calling out to alert everyone he was returning. Couldn't risk friendly fire from that Ruger. The young man remained on the ground, and Nancy crouched beside him, her face white. "He's not responding."

Jock knelt to check the assailant. His pulse was thready, his skin cold and clammy. *Has he overdosed?*

Flashing lights blazed through the café, announcing Chief Anderson's vehicle pulling up out front. Jock's boss jogged up the steps toward them. The short, heavy-framed man had thinning brown hair that he covered with a Cordova PD baseball cap, reminding Jock of the bulldog mascot from his Little League days.

"See you've got things under control here, O'Halloran. Garrison and Miller have gone after the truck." The chief gave him a nod before walking toward Nancy.

Jock wasn't so sure things were under control. He rolled the unconscious man onto his side. His breathing had become depressed, and he was making a strange gurgling sound. Up close he looked little more than a kid. Twenty at most. "I'm calling the paramedics." Jock reached for his radio. "Suspected drug overdose." He read out the address and the symptoms.

The chief came over. "What happened?"

"He came in high as a kite and lunged for Mrs. Tait the moment he saw her." Jock pointed to the knife, which he'd retrieved, bagged and placed safely on the table. "I disarmed him, but I think he might be crashing. The paramedics should be here soon."

"Fentanyl?"

Jock grimaced. "I'd say so. I'll check for identification." Jock pulled on some latex gloves before carefully patting down the man. If he had been injecting the drugs, he might still have a needle on him.

Chief Anderson held the man steady while Jock reached into his pocket, pulling out a wallet to check for ID.

"Ethan Davis." Jock looked at the chief and Phoebe. "Name ring a bell?"

None of them knew the name.

The paramedics arrived and quickly prepared him for transport. They let Jock grab some gloves and wipes so he could treat the cuts on Phoebe's face. Thankfully, they were superficial scratches and would heal quickly without any scarring.

Nancy arrived with their meals in bags. The color had returned to her face. "I figured you'd want these to go now." Tendrils of hair had come loose from her usually neat ponytail, and she regarded the scene with dismay.

"Thank you." Phoebe took both bags, holding them on her lap.

Jock gave her a reassuring smile. "Thanks, Nancy."

The gurney crunched over the broken glass, causing Nancy to sigh. "He sure made a mess."

The chief stepped back to let the paramedics by. "The crime scene tech should be here soon. Until then, you can wait here." He glanced at Nancy. "I know you'd like this cleaned up as soon as possible, but we need to collect evidence."

"I understand." Nancy wandered over to the other patrons, who sat talking among themselves.

Jock frowned. They really should've been separated to take witness statements. That'd require more officers than they had. Thankfully, his testimony and the surveillance footage could do most of the heavy lifting if it came to court.

The chief turned to go, but Jock stopped him. "Chief, can I talk to you a moment?"

"Sure." The chief walked through the door, and Jock followed.

The bracing, salty air hit him in the face, and Jock rubbed his hands together before shoving them in his pockets. "Sir, I take it you read my report about the incidents yesterday?" His breath came out in puffs as it condensed in the frigid air.

The chief nodded. "Good job on stopping the kidnapping. That poor woman must've been beside herself."

"Yes, it was a terrible shock. Thing is, it's possible that Ethan Davis targeted Mrs. Tait, and this along with the other incidents are linked to her husband's case."

"You mean Ronnie Tait? The accidental drowning? I don't follow." The chief straightened his cap.

Jock pressed his lips together. If he didn't convince the chief that the danger posed to Phoebe was linked to her husband's death, he wouldn't reopen the case. "Mrs. Tait found threatening messages on her husband's phone. She couldn't access them while the investigation was ongoing, but I've seen them now. I think they might be connected to his death. After she accessed them, the guy who tried to kidnap her son yesterday started hanging around her house back in Tucson. Someone—probably him—broke into her house. Now he's shooting up the diner?" Jock gestured to the disastrous scene before them.

The chief frowned. "Did you put copies in the file?"

"Yes."

"I'll take a look at them right away. You take statements from the witnesses here." The chief turned to go, interrupting some seagulls that squawked and fought over a few stray fries.

"Sir, after what's just happened, do you think Bruce could stay with my mom and Mrs. Tait's son while I'm on shift? Miller said he has a stack of paperwork, so Bruce would just be sleeping at his feet."

The chief gave him a skeptical look.

Before he could say no, Jock continued, "Otherwise, I think Mrs. Tait will want her son with her." Jock raised his eyebrows, allowing the chief to imagine having a two-year-old running amok in the PD.

The chief blew out a breath. “That dog’s great with little kids. If Miller says yes, have him drop the K-9 off at your mom’s to guard her and the child. Seems likely Mrs. Tait is the intended target. She needs to come back with you.” He grinned. “Marge O’Halloran is armed and dangerous. I think she can handle whatever comes her way.” He brushed a few flakes of snow off his shoulders and walked to his vehicle.

Jock turned his eyes to the sky. *Lord, I hope he’s right.* While his mom might be able to hold her own ordinarily, the people after Phoebe were dangerous. If Phoebe had stumbled upon something bigger than they knew, they could be professionals. Better catch them quickly. He returned to the café where Phoebe ate her fish and chips out of the bag. The aroma made his mouth water.

She looked up, licking her fingers. “I’m not even that hungry anymore—I guess this is what they call stress eating.”

Jock willed his stomach not to growl again. “Keep eating and I’ll be back shortly.” He walked toward Nancy, who gave him her statement and promised to send through her security footage.

“I’m so glad you were here.” Nancy’s emotion-rich voice sent a jolt of anger through Jock’s heart. Whoever had targeted Phoebe was impacting his hometown as well. These people needed to be brought to justice. Hopefully, Ethan Davis would give them some answers. Maybe even the name of the man who’d been attacking Phoebe and Charlie. Garrison and Miller had lost the gray truck, so they were no closer to finding him.

It took half an hour for Jock to finalize the statements, hand the scene over to the crime scene technician, scarf down his lunch and set out toward Cordova PD with

Phoebe. The relentless snow swirled around the car, and his windshield wipers worked overtime.

"I'm worried about Charlie. Could we go check on him?" She wrung her hands, her shoulders tense.

Jock checked the time. "Yes, I understand your concern. It'll have to be a quick visit. Miller should be swinging by to drop off Bruce, so Charlie will be safe."

"Thank you." Phoebe's eyes softened, and Jock's heart along with it. What had this woman been through that made her so grateful for the smallest win?

Jock turned toward his mom's. If he were honest with himself, *he'd* feel better going by too. His mom could handle herself, but after the brazenness of the shooting she needed to be vigilant.

Phoebe ran her fingers through her hair, letting it fall. "Why do you think they sent that man in first, with the knife? It doesn't make sense."

"I've been wondering the same thing. But he wasn't in his right mind. It's possible he didn't follow instructions. He might've just been sent in to confirm you were there."

"Maybe." A few minutes passed before she spoke again. "Do you think Ronnie showed them a photo of me and Charlie?"

"It's possible." If Ronnie had worked with these people, he may have shared some family snaps. But if the attacker had been watching Ronnie's house, he could just as easily have taken photos of Phoebe and Charlie. The thought of someone spying on them chilled Jock, making his stomach harden.

Phoebe rubbed her hands over her face. "I didn't expect any of this. I don't understand why Ronnie's death is so important. I mean, *I* want to find the truth. But he wasn't a high-profile person or anything special. He was just a fisherman. I'm beginning to regret coming here."

Grateful for the natural opening, Jock asked, "Why *did* you come?"

Phoebe rolled her shoulders. "I wasn't getting any help over the phone. Besides, I owe it to Ronnie. As his wife. If I don't find out what really happened, no one else will." She turned to him. "Loyalty is very important to me, but I think I'm reaching my limit."

Jock's breath caught. He understood how she felt. When his stepfather had left them, stealing his mom's savings in the process, he'd vowed to avenge his mom. Thankfully, the Lord had other plans. How he wished he could protect Phoebe from whatever conflicted emotions and pain she was experiencing, but he could not find the words. They pulled into his mom's driveway, and he said the only thing he could think of. "Hopefully seeing Charlie will help."

"It sure can't hurt." She smiled.

Moments later, Phoebe sat on the sofa with Charlie entangled in her arms. "Mama hurt!" The little boy stroked Phoebe's face where the tiny cuts peppered her cheek. "Kiss'em better!"

He gave her some sloppy kisses that made Phoebe's eyes crinkle with joy. "Thanks, buddy! Have you been having fun?"

"Yep!" Charlie stroked Phoebe's hair, looking at her as if she were the only person in the world who mattered.

Marge returned with a tray of hot cocoa. She leaned in and whispered, "I remember when that was you and me."

Jock's heart clenched. How long before he'd lost that innocence? Not as long as it should've been. How he hoped Charlie wouldn't experience that. *That's in the past.* He intended for it to remain there.

A hot cocoa and a car trip later, Jock sat opposite his boss, who had the case file open in front of him with Phoebe's printed messages beside it. He resisted the urge to commentate on the file, instead allowing his boss to read in silence. The frown deepened the further he read. Nervous energy caused Jock's legs to jiggle, and he stilled them.

With a grunt, his boss looked up and nodded at Jock. "I agree with you, O'Halloran. There's a connection there. If these people had something to do with Ronnie Tait's death, we need to know." He stacked the file. "Besides, Garrison did a little detective work based on that plate number. It matches one stolen last week. You go ahead and investigate the whole thing and let me know what you find."

Jock's mouth went dry with relief. "Thanks, Chief." He couldn't wait to tell Phoebe.

Phoebe's emotions were all over the place. She felt exhausted, having barely slept last night. But the adrenaline crash from the young man trying to attack her, then the shooting, left her wired and unable to sit still. Checking up on Charlie had helped. Jock seemed to anticipate what she needed, which put her at ease. His quick thinking and bravery at the café remained in her mind, and she was so thankful he was the officer assigned to her case. He'd known what Charlie needed as well. Officer Miller had dropped off his K-9, Bruce, who had taken an immediate shine to her son. Marge O'Halloran had helped reassure her too. The woman had a heart of solid gold. Phoebe couldn't help but compare the woman to her own mom, who had no patience for anyone under the age of independence.

Marge hadn't dismissed Phoebe's concerns. Quite the opposite. She seemed to intuitively understand her situation and promised to send photo updates every half hour. That had allowed Phoebe to agree to Jock's logic—if Phoebe was the main target, being at the house with Charlie and Marge would put Charlie in more danger.

The problem was, putting anyone in danger seemed selfish now. Her quest for justice stemmed from guilt more than anything else. How could guilt justify the damage her presence here in Cordova was causing? Her guilt that after the first year of marriage, she hadn't loved Ronnie like a wife should. No matter how loving she acted toward him, how much she set aside her own needs in favor of his, the complete lack of reciprocation wore her down until seeds of resentment sprouted. Now he was dead, she struggled to feel animosity toward him. She couldn't when she had Charlie. Instead, guilt had taken over.

Jock exited Chief Anderson's office with a grin on his face, pulling her attention back to the present. "Looks like we're reopening the case."

Phoebe's knees weakened a little as relief washed over her. "Thanks, that's great news." Now that the police had committed to this, she had to see it through. No matter the motivation. She had a chance to get justice for Ronnie.

"I'm just going to print out the stills from the CCTV at the diner that Nancy sent through. Hopefully between those and the stills from the airport, you'll be able to help identify the men." Jock gestured for her to follow him to his desk, where he clicked through to the pictures.

Phoebe examined them on the screen. "Have you tracked down the owner of the truck?"

Jock grabbed the printouts. "Not exactly. The plates were stolen. They match a red GMC Sierra 1500." He raised his eyebrows. "Okay, here we go." He spread the printouts on the desk.

The first picture showed the man grabbing Charlie while

Phoebe wrestled with the stroller. Her gut clenched at the memory. While she'd seen the man's face, the security surveillance only showed his chin, dipped below his baseball cap. "He must've known where the cameras were at the terminal."

"Unfortunately, I think you're right." Jock flipped to the pictures from the diner. "Even here, there's no clear picture. The pictures of Ethan Davis are clear, but the shooter had stayed in the F-150, with only his arm and the shotgun protruding." Jock tapped the photo. "You said he had a buzz cut, slightly sunken eyes, around six feet. Anything else?"

Phoebe thought for a moment. "I think he maybe had brown hair. I didn't get a close look at him, sorry." She pressed her lips together. "My neighbors had CCTV that they gave to the police after the break-in. I didn't get a copy myself. Just didn't think to ask."

"Could you ask now? If they'd be more comfortable sending it directly to me, I can reach out." The softness in Jock's voice made Phoebe's chest tighten.

She licked her lips, pulling out her phone. "Let me find out."

"While you're doing that, I'll check up on Ethan Davis." He stepped away to make the phone call, and Phoebe texted her neighbor. Fortunately, the woman was happy to forward what she'd sent to the Tucson PD directly to Phoebe.

The message arrived as Jock returned. "How did it go?"

Phoebe pressed Play on the video and held it up so Jock could watch with her. The footage was from across the road, but was shot in high definition. A man with exactly the same body shape as the attacker slipped across the sidewalk and jumped Phoebe's fence.

"That's him!" Phoebe pointed to the man then sped up the footage. Soon, he returned, slipping back to the sidewalk empty-handed. Phoebe scrolled back and paused on the footage. "I can't see his face. Can you?"

Jock squinted then gently took the phone from Phoebe, pinching the screen to see if he could enlarge the image. "The baseball cap hides it. All I can see is his chin. Just like the airport footage." He clicked his tongue in frustration. "Did the police check any other footage from along the street?"

"I don't think so. Ronnie and I hadn't been in the area long. I only know the neighbors immediately adjacent to our house, so I wouldn't know how to contact them." Phoebe tried not to let her shoulders sag. Wasn't *their* house anymore. Just hers. She'd have to try harder with the neighbors when she returned.

"I can reach out to the Tucson PD." Jock frowned, thinking aloud. "He was acting alone, unless there was a driver somewhere in the vicinity. Didn't look like he'd taken anything. If he'd planned to steal something bigger than he could carry in his hands, he would've had to bring a vehicle." His phone buzzed, and he checked it. His shoulders slumped as he read the message.

Phoebe's stomach lurched. Could it be a problem with Charlie? "Is everything okay?"

"Just that update about Ethan Davis." Jock gave her arm a reassuring squeeze.

"Oh." Phoebe allowed herself to relax again. Nothing to do with Charlie. "Is he okay?"

"He's hanging in there, but they've had to put him in an induced coma." Jock pursed his lips. "It's not a good sign."

"I guess we need to try and find some more witnesses, then, huh?" Phoebe straightened her shoulders.

Jock raised his eyebrows. "Exactly. You're good at this."

Phoebe willed away the tinge of pink creeping up her cheeks. "It's just common sense." But the praise felt nice.

They spent the next couple of hours comparing Phoebe's notes with what Jock had found in Ronnie's file. Jock emailed the Tucson PD to ask them to send their file on the break-in.

Moments later, his phone rang. "It's my mom. You can listen too." Jock answered on speaker. "Is everything okay?"

"Hey, hon, Bruce is growling."

Jock stood, beckoning for Phoebe to follow him. "Are you and Charlie okay?" They hustled toward the front of the station.

Phoebe's palms became clammy. *Why did I agree to leave Charlie?*

"We're both fine, thanks. It's just Bruce. He'd been snoozing, then he jumped to his feet, growling, and headed for the back door."

Phoebe leaped into the front seat, and Jock started the engine. "We'll be there soon, just stay where you are and stay on the line."

"I smell smoke." Marge's tone changed. "Charlie, let's go over here."

Phoebe's pulse raced, and she turned toward Jock. *"Smoke?"*

Jock gave her a reassuring look, already accelerating as fast as was safe. He grabbed his radio. "Dispatch, I need the fire department." He gave out his mom's address. "Mom, where's it coming from?"

"I don't know. It's not from the kitchen, and I don't light the fire in here until the sun sets. Maybe that's what Bruce is all caught up about. I'll go check out back."

"No, stay where you are!" Jock's obvious frustration surprised Phoebe. Did he expect his mom to obey him?

Marge didn't seem like the type of woman to take orders from anyone.

"I'm not going to sit around and wait for the house to burn down around us." Marge's tone was stern, and Phoebe hoped the woman knew what she was doing. "It's okay, Charlie, stay near me and Bruce." Her tone changed, reassuring the little boy. Thankfully, he wasn't crying, though it took all her willpower not to grab the phone from Jock and demand Marge put her son on so she could hear his voice.

Dispatch crackled through on Jock's radio with an update.

"Mom, the fire department will be there in ten minutes. We'll be there in five. Don't leave the house unless you need to."

"Are you serious?" Marge's frustration matched her son's.

Jock grimaced. "There may be someone outside waiting to shoot at you. If you need to evacuate, go out the back. Head for the tree line."

A loud banging came through the speaker, and Phoebe gasped.

"What's happening?" Concern replaced the frustration in Jock's voice.

Phoebe's stomach churned, and she clasped her hands in her lap.

"Someone's at the front door." Marge's voice sounded distant, like she'd taken the phone away from her ear.

"Do *not* answer it, Mom." Jock pinched his lips together

Marge tsked. "Bad guys don't knock on doors, Jock. It's probably a neighbor come to help."

Bruce's woof in the background did nothing to still the fear in Phoebe's gut. How she wished Jock could drive faster!

"Oh, it's just Caroline." Marge's voice returned to the phone. "I'll put you on speakerphone."

A woman's rough voice, presumably Caroline's, said something indecipherable.

"Do you know her?" Phoebe was past caring whether she sounded rude to Marge. The feeling of being so far away from her son was gnawing at her like a persistent, dull ache.

Jock gave out a grunt. "She owns the inn you were supposed to be staying at."

"The ex-navy woman?" Phoebe's breath hitched. Surely having someone with a military background was a good thing.

"Yes." Jock and Marge spoke over each other.

"She's my friend, Phoebe, don't worry. We're going to head outside, Jock. I don't like this." Marge sounded breathless. "Caroline, grab the fire extinguisher."

"Mom, just evacuate. Leave the firefighting to the experts." Jock gripped the steering wheel hard enough to turn his knuckles white.

Phoebe's eyes stung. "If anything happens to Charlie..."

"I won't let it." The determined confidence in Marge's voice did a little to help, but not much.

"We'll be there in two minutes. Like I said before, if you evacuate, head for the tree line and seek cover." Jock had to slow for the snowplow that ground its way toward them.

The call dropped, and Jock redialed. Straight to voicemail.

Phoebe's blood pressure rose. She wanted to yell at the driver to get out of the way. "Why isn't she answering?"

Jock placed his hand on her arm. "Just keep praying. That man hasn't harmed Charlie before—I don't think he'll hurt him now. But he might try to take him again."

Keep praying? Phoebe let out a sob. God hadn't answered her earlier prayers—what made her imagine He'd answer this? She was too far gone for Him to hear her. Still, maybe it'd make her feel better. She dipped her head. *Lord, please protect Charlie.*

Jock gave her arm a squeeze beforc accelerating past the snowplow. "I'm more worried about my mom. She'd take a bullet before she let anything happen to your son. Now Caroline's there, it'll be harder for him to act." He pressed the accelerator to the floor. "We'll be there soon."

They turned into Marge's driveway to see thick smoke billowing from the rear of the house. Thankfully, no flames appeared to be within the house. Yet. Phoebe's heart ached for the lovely home Marge had created, that could all be gone. Because Phoebe let them convince her to leave her son. Never again.

Jock pulled out of the way, presumably to allow the fire truck access. They swung their doors open in unison, and woodsmoke mixed with gasoline filled Phoebe's nostrils.

"Charlie!" Phoebe raced toward the house. But a loud *bang* came from behind. Bullets kicked up the snow next to her feet, and she instinctively dived behind the police vehicle.

"Phoebe!" Jock's distress came through. Where was he?

She didn't bother to look and, instead, scuttled back to the front of the vehicle, away from the bullets that continued to blast around them, pinging off the body of the SUV.

Jock reached her, pulling her into his chest to shield her as he radioed for backup.

Tears pricked Phoebe's eyes. No sign of Marge. *What if Charlie's hurt?*

FOUR

Jock's heart pounded in his chest. The shots came from the neighbor's front yard, behind a copse of spruce trees. Must've lit the fire to get Phoebe back to the house. *Lord, please help us. Protect Charlie and Mom too.* He didn't want to risk firing back in case he accidentally shot someone else—there was a chance the attacker had already taken Charlie. He could be using his mom or Caroline as a human shield. Jock needed to keep Phoebe safe until backup arrived.

"Hang in there." He clasped Phoebe to him as more shots fired, impacting his vehicle so violently that it vibrated and rocked.

Phoebe gave a whimper in response. She must be terrified. He dialed his mom's phone again. This time the call didn't even go through. Could the attacker be using a cell phone jammer?

The attacker knew exactly where they were. Calling out to his mom would at least give him an idea of the situation. No, not his mom.

Jock took a deep breath, projecting his voice as best he could. "Bruce! Speak!"

Bruce's whining barks filled the air, and Jock breathed a sigh of relief. The barks came from out back. The K-9 wouldn't leave the side of his mom or Charlie unless he'd been incapacitated, or Miller released him. Barks suggested he remained by their side. Phoebe seemed to relax a little beside him. Maybe she'd come to the same conclusion.

Jock pushed Phoebe behind him and edged around the vehicle toward the attacker, his weapon raised. If he could just get off one shot…

Bang! Another round fired toward him, narrowly missing his shoulder. Jock pulled back. The attacker must have some kind of scope. No way he could get a clean shot without a distraction. *Lord, I sure could use Your help.*

The welcome sounds of the fire truck's siren echoed toward them. *Thank You, Lord.* Their attacker wouldn't stick around for long now. Jock pressed Phoebe into him. "Stay close. He might try again."

Phoebe didn't move, and they waited as the sirens grew closer. The sounds of an engine starting and tires spinning against gravel had Jock on his feet. The gray truck accelerated past his mom's driveway, and Jock fired, emptying his clip into the vehicle. He smashed out the side window and managed to hit the rear tire. The vehicle swerved as the tire blew out, but corrected, driving on. He radioed in the update, praying that someone would finally catch up with the attacker. Phoebe had already broken away from the vehicle, crunching through the snowdrifts toward the side of the house.

"Wait for me." Jock shook his head, racing after her. His cell phone rang. *Mom.* He answered. "Hold your fire. We're coming to you!"

He rounded the side of the house, where snowdrifts were tinged gray with particulate from the fire. The smell of burning paint and wood overpowered his senses, and he pressed a glove to cover his nose and mouth. Phoebe's smoke-shrouded silhouette was halfway across the backyard to his mom, Bruce and Charlie. Thankfully, his mom had taken his advice and remained on the tree line, shotgun in hand, upwind from the smoke.

Caroline had already returned to the house, fire extinguisher in hand, working on the fire. Flames flickered at the corner of the back porch, where a small woodpile had been neatly stacked, ready to bring into the house. Even in the freezing conditions, the logs were dry and burned brightly. Fire leaped up the wall and licked the porch roof, hissing and cracking. If they didn't put it out, it would take hold in the roof.

Jock's eyes widened, and he rushed toward Caroline. "Did the flames enter the house?"

Caroline turned, tossing the fire extinguisher to the side and reaching for the fire blanket. "I don't know."

"Here, give me that, go get some air in your lungs." Jock grabbed the fire blanket from Caroline and held it in front of his face, shielding himself from the radiant heat. Caroline stepped off the back porch and into the snow, coughing.

Before he could make much use of the fire blanket, firemen tramped into view, carrying heavy equipment. *That was quick.*

The fire chief approached Jock. "You're done here. Is there anyone inside?"

"No." Jock backed off the porch and jogged toward the gathered women, gasping for fresh air. "Are you okay?"

Phoebe held her son, and Marge stroked Bruce's neck. Caroline mopped her sweaty brow with a handkerchief.

"I think we're okay, aren't we, Charlie?" Marge grinned at the toddler, who grinned back.

Jock breathed a sigh of relief. "We can talk about what

happened when the fire's out." He stepped away to call Chief Anderson. Hopefully, they'd managed to catch the guy.

Before long, the fire truck was packed up and ready to go. The fire damage to the house had been superficial, so they'd all gathered back inside.

Chief Morrow's heavy boots clomped over what remained of the porch. He poked his head into the kitchen to summon Jock and Miller, who'd come to assist and retrieve his K-9.

They stepped outside, and the chief updated them as they walked him back to the truck. "The fire was deliberately lit. Whoever did it used gasoline, and they threw the can into the fire, so it's burned up pretty well. Go ahead and bag what you need to, and I'll send you a report."

"Thanks, Pete. We'll take care of it," Officer Miller said.

"Anything out of the ordinary?" Jock barely contained his frustration.

"Honestly, Marge should be thankful. They could've used a full can of gas, but I'd say whatever can they used must've been fairly empty. The trail was short, and there was a lot less fuel than I'd expect if someone wanted to burn the house down quickly."

Officer Miller said, "We can be thankful for that."

"Thanks, Chief," Jock murmured. His findings pointed toward the likelihood that the fire had been designed to lure Phoebe to the house.

Chief Morrow climbed into the fire truck, started the engine, then backed down the driveway.

Jock followed Miller and Bruce over to inspect the damage to his vehicle.

"Do you think it's drivable?" Jock crouched to examine the passenger side. It'd sustained some shotgun damage, but the door opened okay.

Miller shook his head. "Nothing the panel beater can't patch. Those windows need attention, though."

Jock pulled off his hat, running his fingers through his hair before replacing it. "I don't understand how he got away. His tire's blown out, and it's virtually impossible to drive like that. Not in this weather."

"He probably dumped it. You think he has help?" Miller allowed Bruce to sniff the vehicle.

"Maybe. He had that kid, Ethan Davis. There may be others." Jock glanced back at the house. "I should go check on everyone."

"I'll wait around and drive you back into town." Miller walked toward his vehicle, Bruce at his heels.

Jock jogged to the house, letting himself in the front. He found Phoebe in the kitchen, holding Charlie. The little boy had his fist wrapped around a chunk of his mom's famous tea cake. The bunny tucked under his arm looked a little worse for wear, with a few smudges of soot on his ears. The crumbs on a plate in front of Caroline suggested she'd just finished hers. Marge held a cup of tea in both hands, her eyes fixed on Charlie.

Jock's heart felt heavy as he regarded Phoebe and her son. Thankfully, Charlie seemed perfectly fine. Jock felt responsible for them in a way he hadn't for other victims of crime, and he couldn't explain why. Better to keep his mind on track. He'd questioned Caroline, and Miller had questioned Jock's mom, but neither added information they didn't already know. Though Caroline hadn't had much to say. He didn't know the woman as well as his mom did, but she'd always seemed to keep to herself.

He stepped into the kitchen, and Caroline turned to him. "Now that I think of it, I might've seen a gray truck turn into the McKenzies' place."

Phoebe's shoulders tensed, and she cradled Charlie a little tighter.

Jock set his jaw. Why hadn't Caroline mentioned it before? "Did you get the make and model?"

"Ford F-150." Caroline pursed her lips, her eyes flicking to Phoebe. "Is it safe for you to stay here? Do you have anyone back home who might be able to keep you safe there?"

"Caroline—" Marge's tone seemed likely to escalate into a defense of Phoebe.

Color rose in Phoebe's cheeks. "You're right, Caroline. While I'm glad I didn't put you in any more danger by staying at the inn, I've brought it here instead. I'm so sorry, Marge. I never should've made Charlie your responsibility."

Marge reached over, giving her a reassuring pat on the shoulder. "This is not your fault, and don't for one second feel guilty about it. As for Charlie, it's my absolute pleasure to care for this sweet little fellow." She gave Charlie an impish smile, pinching his cheek.

The child reciprocated, giving a giggle when Marge pretended to be shocked as his chubby paw came toward her.

"Do you know who wants to hurt you?" Caroline crossed her arms, ignoring Marge and Charlie's antics. Instead, she observed Phoebe with curiosity.

Jock's stomach tensed, and he opened his mouth to tell Caroline he'd be the one asking the questions. But his mom beat him to it.

"Leave the poor girl alone." Marge shook her head.

"It's okay." Phoebe retrieved a scrap of cake Charlie had dropped, popping it back on the plastic plate in front of him. "I don't know if justice is worth putting other people in danger."

Jock crossed his arms. "That's not—"

Caroline interrupted. "I can understand your hesitation.

Who knows what they'll try next. You or Charlie might be killed…"

"Caroline—" Jock's temperature rose.

Marge gave Caroline a stern look, interrupting him again. "Let's not overdramatize things. This isn't one of your naval battles that warrants a tactical retreat. It's one guy with some screws loose who, among other things, has tried to burn down my house and kidnap a defenseless child. Whatever his reason, he needs to be taken off the streets. The sooner the better! Isn't that right, Jock?" Jock wasn't about to correct her. He hadn't filled her in on every detail, and obviously neither had Phoebe.

"Yes." He caught Phoebe's eye. "Are you ready to go?"

This time, he'd take Charlie and his mom with him. Find them somewhere safer to stay. *Where that might be, I don't know.*

Phoebe suddenly felt weak. When Marge put it that way, the weight of obligation lowered on her shoulders. She had to see this to the end. To make sure that the culprits wouldn't hurt anyone else. How she wished she could take it to the Lord, like she used to. Like she'd done since she gave herself to Him just after her twelfth birthday. But when Ronnie became the center of her life, she'd put any conversation with the Lord on the back burner. Did she deserve to ask Him for help now? Would He even take her back? Based on her recent prayers, it didn't bode well. *At least He listens to Jock.* The officer seemed to take his relationship with the Lord for granted, like he truly saw the Lord as his Father. How Phoebe longed for that easy trust.

Jock's eyes remained on hers, and she realized his question hung in the air. She wasn't ready to go anywhere. But they couldn't stay here.

"I have to get going." Caroline stood. "I'll let myself out."

Marge gave Caroline a hug. "Thanks for your help, as always. Don't know what I'd do without you."

Caroline smiled a little awkwardly, and Jock stepped to the side to let her past.

"Mom—"

"Don't start. I've had a long day, and I need to wash away the smoke before I call Ben Timmins for a quote to repair my porch. Hopefully, he can get here today."

Jock's eyes widened. "Mom, I need to bring you—"

"I know you're enthusiastic with a hammer, son, but Ben's a professional." Marge may as well have dusted her hands off, putting the subject to rest.

Jock briefly closed his eyes and waited for his mom to walk by him. "Pack a bag, Mom."

Phoebe used the moment to examine him more closely. He'd removed his hat, tucking it into his pocket. His hair had been mussed, and a smear of ash colored his cheek. His uniform needed a wash where he must've wiped some ash from his hands. Would he shed some light on his mom's comment about his handyman skills? She didn't plan to ask.

He glanced at Phoebe and gave her a conspiratorial grin. "She's probably right about my poor carpentry skills, but don't tell her that." He ran his hand through his hair, making its mussed state worse. "I need to get you all somewhere safer than here."

Phoebe's throat ached a little, and she reached for the untouched tea that Marge had poured her. "I should pack a bag for Charlie." They had their suitcase, but lugging that around the station wasn't efficient. Charlie needed his own little backpack refreshed with a change of clothes and some snacks.

After Phoebe and Marge had each packed a bag, Miller

drove them to Cordova PD. Marge had found a car seat for Charlie—the one she used for her grandson when he visited from Florida. Phoebe rode in back with Charlie and Bruce, while Marge rode shotgun. Jock followed up the rear in his damaged but drivable vehicle. The fire department had investigated and bagged evidence from the fire, but the crime scene technician wouldn't make it before the inclement weather came. So they'd taken some photos, bagged the bullets, and decided that driving it back to the station was the better option.

Marge had agreed to come to the PD only to look after Charlie, but she refused to remain away from her home. She had the repairman coming to fix the porch, before the inclement weather arrived, and she wanted to supervise. Reading between the lines, Phoebe suspected Marge had a more than professional interest in this repairman. Probably best to keep that observation to herself. Charlie and Marge headed for the break room, while Jock and Phoebe returned to Jock's desk.

Jock fixed his eyes on his computer screen and raised his eyebrows. "Sorry to tell you, Phoebe, the threatening messages sent to Ronnie are a dead end." He pointed to his screen. "Looks like even the techies couldn't track their source."

"That's a shame." The weight on Phoebe grew a little heavier. Would they ever find the people responsible? If they hadn't caught him already, it seemed unlikely they ever would.

Before Jock could say anything further, Miller stopped by his desk. Bruce trotted at his heels. "I tracked down the registered owner of the fishing boat for you. Do you want me to give him a call, or leave it with you?"

Bruce nosed Jock's pocket. Jock slipped him a treat. "Thanks, I'll call him now."

Phoebe couldn't help but smile. The man seemed to be brimming with treats, whether for canines, toddlers or even her. He gave them freely, seemingly just for the enjoyment of those around him. She hadn't seen him eat any himself.

Miller handed him the details, and Phoebe recognized the name of the captain of the boat on which her husband had met his death. "Come on, Bruce."

Jock gave Phoebe a sympathetic look. "These are details about the fishing boat Ronnie was working on when he died." He checked Miller's notes. "Doesn't tell us anything new. Except to say the owner primarily docks it in Cordova." He grabbed his phone. "I'll give him a call. You may as well listen in."

Phoebe's knees weakened. How grateful she was to be included without a fight.

Jock dialed the number, putting it on speaker. Hopefully questioning the man in light of the new information would offer something the original investigating officers had overlooked.

A gruff voice answered on the fifth ring. "John Kemp."

"Captain Kemp, this is Officer Jock O'Halloran from the Cordova Police Department. I'm calling about your boat." Jock read the registration details to the man.

Kemp hesitated before answering. "Yeah, that's mine. Somethin' happened to it?"

"It's part of an ongoing investigation."

Kemp coughed, then cleared his throat. "What investigation?"

Jock raised his eyebrows at Phoebe. "We need to examine your boat, sir. How about you come to the station, and we can discuss it." From what she'd learned about police procedure, Jock had no grounds to compel the man to cooperate.

"Ah, no can do, Officer. It's Dungeness crab season. I'm down in Oregon, back in March for halibut. Can't it wait till then?" His breath sounded shallow, and Phoebe guessed he'd be sweating.

Jock paused. "Sir, if we have to impound your boat, it might not be ready by March."

"Impound?" Kemp spluttered. "What are you talkin' about, impound? Don't you need a warrant or somethin'?"

Jock's pursed his lips. "If we check it out now, we can clear this whole thing up. You have nothing to hide, do you?"

"Ah, I have nothin' to hide. What's this about, anyway? What investigation?" Kemp's voice raised a little, his suspicion obvious.

Jock glanced at Phoebe. "Ronnie Tait's death."

Kemp scoffed. "Tait's death was ruled an accident. You…you go ahead. Get a warrant." He hung up.

Adrenaline rushed through Phoebe. "He doesn't seem to care!"

Jock placed a hand on her arm. "He has something to hide, for sure. Notice he said it was *ruled* an accident. Not that it *was* an accident."

Phoebe's palms grew hot. She took a deep breath, trying to calm herself. Jock had a point.

"But it *is* strange he doesn't seem concerned. I was expecting him to be more flustered, not less, when I mentioned Ronnie. I need to get that search warrant." Jock looked her directly in the eye.

The fact that Jock remained calm helped to calm Phoebe too. He had things under control. He'd get to the bottom of it. Unlike many, he cared.

He turned to his computer, but his phone rang. "It's

the hospital's main line." He answered, this time without switching to speaker. "O'Halloran."

Phoebe strained to hear the other end of the conversation but failed.

"That's correct." He listened. Then his shoulders drooped. Must be bad news. Jock clenched his teeth. "We'll need to collect the physical phone, but yes, that'd be great if you could send them through. Thanks for that." His phone pinged. "Thanks, Ashley."

Jock ended the call, then checked his messages.

Phoebe peered over his shoulder. The photos were from Ethan Davis's phone. Multiple messages taken from a locked screen. The sender had used *precede* when they meant *proceed*. The same mistake in the threatening messages sent to Ronnie.

Precede to the meeting point.

Where are you?

Call me.

Jock looked up at Phoebe, his face serious. "It looks like Ethan was working for the same people as Ronnie."

Phoebe's face dropped. "Do you think there are others like him?"

"I sure hope so, because Ethan Davis was pronounced dead twenty minutes ago."

Phoebe's mouth fell open. First Ronnie, now Ethan. Who else had to die before they solved the case?

Jock's mind raced. The hospital had found Ethan Davis's phone in his shoe. If he hadn't handed him off to the paramedics, he and the chief would've found it, and they could've been working on it already. Too bad. With Ethan Davis dead, any information he knew had died with him. Jock needed to re-interview everyone else involved in Ronnie Tait's case as soon as possible.

Phoebe gave a deep sigh. "That's a shame. He was so young."

Jock's heart rate picked up as he watched her. The young man might have tried to stab her, but she seemed genuinely sorry he'd died. "We got his phone, so we'll check it for leads." He rubbed his hands on his legs, leaning toward her.

Phoebe drew in a sharp breath. "You know what, look for messages from his friend, Kyle Smith. I didn't think about it before, but Kyle might've known Ronnie's friends. He'd go stay with him sometimes."

"Does he live here in Cordova?"

"I think he was fly in, fly out, like Ronnie. But I didn't have much to do with him. You'll be able to track him down. His details are on my phone." Phoebe fished out her phone and clicked on the relevant folder of screenshots. "Here." She handed it to Jock. "I'd have given it to you before, but it wasn't relevant at the time."

Jock read through the messages, his jaw ticking. Just male banter. Nothing special. But the way Ronnie referred to Phoebe was belittling at best. "Do you think they spent a lot of time together in person?"

Phoebe frowned. "Ronnie didn't tell me much about anything, I'm afraid."

He continued reading, even as sympathy welled in his heart. How could a man keep so much from his wife and talk about her with such disdain? No wonder she seemed so starved of compliments. Must've been thin on the ground at home. Wouldn't surprise him if Ronnie Tait was emotionally abusive. Phoebe deserved so much better. "Do you mind if I send these to my phone?"

"That's fine." She bit her bottom lip.

"I'll feed them into the timeline, and we can see what comes up. Feel free to check on Charlie while I'm doing that, if you want."

"Thanks." Phoebe didn't hesitate, hightailing it to her son.

Jock pulled up the timeline he'd prepared, then stopped. Clicking away and into the database, he typed in Kyle's details. While it was helpful to have Phoebe around, he'd rather check up on Ronnie's associates without her. For all he knew, Kyle might have a criminal record a mile long. Better not to give Phoebe more worry until absolutely necessary.

The file came up right away. Assault, criminal damage, a few misdemeanors. Though none were earlier than ten years ago, and all in Chicago. Maybe Kyle had moved away from a bad crowd and turned his life around. Current address was in Cordova. *So not FIFO.* Had Ronnie lied about that? Anyway, it made sense for Ronnie to stay with Kyle if he had a room free. He jotted down the details and reached for his phone. Might as well find out if he could come in for an interview.

Straight to voicemail. Jock left a message and noted it on the file, then added the dates from Kyle's messages into the timeline.

He finished just as Phoebe walked back into the room. "How's Charlie doing?"

Phoebe smiled. "Fine. Going a little stir crazy, but your mom is amazing with him."

"Yeah, she spends as much time as she can with Wallace's son." He missed Wallace and her son.

"She's your sister, isn't she?" Phoebe gazed at him with focus.

Jock's chest expanded. "Yes. Paul—my nephew—is a little younger than Charlie. Mom misses him a lot. Like I said, you can see why it's no trouble for her to have you stay."

"I'm beginning to understand." She peered at the screen. "This is the timeline you mentioned?"

"Yeah. The chief suggested I work this as a cold case. So I've put what we know from Ronnie's death until now." He pointed out the incidents, including the man outside Phoebe's house in Tucson, the break-in, the attempted kidnap, the near miss with the gray truck, Ethan Davis's attack, the shooting, Ethan's death and the fire and shooting at his mom's. He'd included the brief notes from Phoebe too.

Jock pointed to the period before Ronnie's death. "You can see here, the lead-up to his death. The circumstances are still unclear. That's what we need to focus on now. I was just about to input Kyle's messages, but maybe you explain what Ronnie told you about his job first? That might shed a little more light on that." No need to tell her Ronnie may have lied about Kyle's living situation. Wouldn't help to make her feel worse.

Phoebe nervously licked her lips. "He worked as a fisherman. Um, the fishing vessel operated offshore, out in deep water. I think usually long lining, but he didn't really go into details."

"Do you have specific dates for when he went away, and when he came home?" Jock's hand remained on the mouse.

"Yeah, they're in my calendar. She fished out her phone, brought up the calendar and placed it on the desk. "I just blocked out when he was away. It's all there in the light blue color." She grimaced. "Ronnie's favorite color."

Jock scrolled through the calendar, keying the dates into the timeline. "This is really helpful. Thanks."

Phoebe's cheeks turned pink, making Jock's chest heavy.

What little encouragement she needed before she blushed. He softened his gaze. "Must've been hard, those long stretches alone."

"I'm pretty independent." Phoebe leaned forward, looking at the timeline.

Jock's phone rang, and he immediately recognized the number. "It's Kyle Smith." He answered. "Officer O'Halloran."

"Officer, you called me." Kyle Smith's tone had a little bit of bravado. Interesting he didn't seem concerned about being called by the police.

"Thank you for returning my call. I would like to come and speak with you. Are you in town?"

Kyle paused. "What's this about?"

Jock had hoped he wouldn't have to alert the man to the subject matter, but there was no way around it if he wanted to interview him. "Ronnie Tait."

"Never heard of him." The man didn't respond too quickly. Didn't take his time. Not obviously lying. *Interesting.*

"What about the name Ethan Davis?"

He paused. "Maybe familiar, but I can't place him. Davis is a common name."

Jock raised his eyebrows. "Okay. Could we talk in person, please?"

"What's the point? I don't know these guys." Kyle's voice remained neutral, almost disinterested.

No way did Jock have grounds to compel the man to come in for an interview. He'd have to try and get the information from him over the phone. "We found some messages on Ronnie Tait's phone from your phone number."

"Huh." Kyle didn't sound worried.

"Are you sure you don't know him? Maybe you knew him by another name." Jock figured he could give the man an out.

After all, he needed whatever information the man might have, and he'd never appeared in the original case file. Also, he hadn't seen Kyle use Ronnie's name in the messages.

"Maybe. Could you send me his photo?" The man sounded curious more than anything.

"No, but I can bring it to you to check."

Kyle sighed. "I don't see what the big deal is."

Jock checked the time. "If you're at home, I can be there in five minutes."

"I guess, sure. You're wasting your time, though. I don't know anyone called Ronnie Tait." Kyle hung up.

"What did he say?" Phoebe rushed her words.

"That he's never heard of your husband." Jock grabbed his jacket.

Her eyes narrowed. "Really?"

"I'll be back soon." He walked toward Miller, who sat doing paperwork with Bruce at his feet. "You good to drive? I have to interview a suspect." No way he'd be going alone.

"I want to come too." Phoebe had followed him.

"No, not this time. You're safe here. Go spend some time with Charlie." Jock's heart twinged at the slight look of disappointment on Phoebe's face. Why did this woman affect him so much?

"Okay." She forced a smile.

Five minutes later, Miller pulled up in front of a slightly run-down, gray weatherboard house. A gray Tacoma was parked in the driveway.

"Let's get this done." Jock headed up the steps, onto the porch, and knocked on the door. A slight aroma of tobacco wafted toward him.

Miller followed up the rear with Bruce. "You think this guy's dangerous?"

"I don't know." Jock kept his hand near his gun, just in case.

A large, hairy man with meaty hands and a five o'clock shadow opened the door, a cigarette hanging from his mouth. He wore a flannel shirt over his thermals. Slightly grubby sheepskin boots covered his feet and ankles. "You must be Officer O'Halloran." He stepped out onto the porch, blowing smoke away from the officers.

"I'm Officer Miller." Miller inclined his head toward the man, stepping out of the snowflakes. Bruce gave a sharp sneeze, shaking the snow out of his fur. Must be the smoke.

"You said that you didn't know Ronnie Tait, but Mr. Tait's wife believes that you were close friends." Jock held out a picture of Ronnie Tait on his phone. "Did you spend time with this man?"

Kyle gave them an incredulous stare. "Randy? Yeah, of course I knew him. He used to stay here all the time. Until…" His face dropped. "I guess that's why you're here? I thought it was an accident."

"How often did he stay?" Jock kept his voice neutral, although inside he felt relieved. Finally, they were getting somewhere.

"Whenever he wasn't out on the water." His subdued tone matched his distant stare. He ran his hands through his hair. "I can't believe his name's Ronnie. No one called him that."

Jock noted that down. Maybe he'd get more information from witnesses with Ronnie's nickname. "You didn't know his surname?"

"Look, I just knew him as Randy." Kyle frowned.

"Do you remember specific dates that he stayed?" Jock poised his pen over his notepad.

Kyle shrugged, leaning against the wall. "I could probably work it out if I had to, but I didn't keep a record. He just came and went whenever. A few guys did. That's why I got this place. Cheaper than the inn, and I like the town."

"We'll follow up on that with you later." He made a note. "When Ronnie and you were together, did you overhear any conversations with colleagues, or meet any of his coworkers?" Jock wasn't confident, given the man didn't even know Ronnie's real name.

"Sure, there were a few. You have someone specific in mind?" The man took a last drag on his dwindling cigarette then stubbed it out under his boot.

"Just anyone from his crew." Jock licked his lips, aware of the cold.

Kyle rubbed his chin. "There was this one guy who showed up once when Randy wasn't expecting him, you know? I thought there was going to be a full-on brawl."

"Did you get his name?" Jock leaned forward, grateful the cigarette was finished.

Kyle frowned, as if trying to remember. "I didn't pay a lot of attention. But Randy might've called him Joe? Moe?" He shrugged, then stooped as a bout of coughing overtook him. When he'd finished, he continued. "I asked him if he needed help, you know. I don't want something kicking off in my place. But he left, said it was just someone from work. I didn't think much of it after that. He never came back."

"What did they talk about?" Jock took a few notes. He could circle back to the man's appearance later.

Kyle blew out a breath, and the stale smell made Jock want to take a step back. "I wasn't eavesdropping or anything."

"Just anything you remember." Jock glanced at Bruce, who sat next to Miller, his nose twitching.

"The guy raised his voice, and Randy raised his. Said something like 'It's dangerous.' And the guy was like 'You don't have a choice.' Then I think Randy might've told him it was the last time. Oh, I remember what he said last, because he yelled it at Randy then left. 'You're done when I say you're done.' I was glad he left."

They had to track down the man. "How did Ronnie—Randy—seem when the man left?"

Kyle crossed his arms, looking between Jock and Miller. "Listen, man, how am I supposed to know? I'm not his mom." He patted his pocket then pulled out a half-empty box of cigarettes and a lighter.

"What did the man look like?" Jock asked.

"About six feet, probably two hundred pounds—pudgy. Sunken, dark brown eyes." Kyle sucked on his new cigarette as he lit it. "Shifty kinda guy. Wouldn't want to meet him alone in a dark alley, you know?" He blew out a new cloud of smoke, making Bruce sneeze again.

Jock wished he could high-five Miller. The man matched the description of the driver of the gray truck. Finally, a solid lead.

"Could you identify him if you saw him again?" Another eyewitness would help a lot.

Kyle did not look happy about the prospect. "I guess."

Jock asked a few more follow-up questions and showed Kyle a picture of Ethan Davis. He didn't recognize him.

Bruce whined, and Miller backed off the porch. "What is it boy?"

"It's okay, boy. We're done. I didn't enjoy those cigarettes either." Jock turned to walk back to the vehicle, and Miller followed. Bruce gave a low growl, nosing Miller in the thigh.

But before they could recognize the K-9's warning, a gunshot broke the quiet.

FIVE

Jock dived for cover as Kyle dropped to the ground—a bullet through his skull. A flock of gulls flew away in alarm, issuing a cacophony of low, piercing caws. The impact jarred Jock's bruised shoulder, and he winced in pain. Rolling onto his stomach, he faced the direction of the gunman. His Glock in hand, he scanned the surroundings. No movement. Had the attacker concealed himself in the neighbor's yard? A thick hedge bordered the property, acting as a fence. He could've fired through or over that.

"Shots fired! One civilian down." Miller radioed in, his voice controlled but urgent. He and Bruce crouched behind the steps, the K-9 low to the ground. Miller and Jock made eye contact, indicating to each other that they remained unscathed.

Would the attacker continue to fire at police? He'd already hit his target. This close to town, it'd be a risk to linger.

Jock's eyes darted around, trying to gauge whether the shooter still posed a threat. He gritted his teeth. Waiting wouldn't help anyone, especially Kyle—if he remained alive. Jock picked up a handful of snow and tossed it toward the hedge. Nothing. Surely if the shooter remained, he would've taken a shot.

His radio crackled. Backup was on the way. Adrenaline pumped through his bloodstream as the seconds stretched. Felt like longer than the minute it'd probably been. Enough time for the shooter to zero in on their position. *Or flee.* Jock crawled along on his stomach, straining to hear the telltale sound of a rifle bolt. Still nothing. Where had the assailant gone? Had he decided to target Kyle then get away while he could? Sirens sounded in the distance, and Jock risked rising slightly from the ground. Nothing. *Lord, thank You for protecting us.*

"I think he's gone." Miller's quiet voice echoed his thoughts. "Bruce, seek."

The K-9 trotted off, headed for the neighbor's bushes, and Miller crouched next to Jock. "Check on the victim?"

Jock nodded, heading for Kyle Smith. Snowflakes continued to drift down, coating the ground and chilling Jock's ears. While he suspected Kyle Smith had died the moment that bullet hit him, there was also a chance he'd survived.

This time, the attacker hadn't used a shotgun, but a rifle. *Might be a hunter.* He'd add that to the profile. He raced up the steps, only to be confronted by an obviously dead Kyle Smith. A bullet had smashed through his skull. Still, he bent to check the man for a pulse. Nothing. He radioed in the update. No rush on the paramedics, but the crime scene techs would need to come before the snow picked up.

"I'm going after Miller." After the relentless attacks, there was no way he'd let Miller face the gunman without backup.

Jock stamped through the snowdrifts to the hedged bushes, following Bruce's and Miller's steps. He rounded the bushes through which Bruce had disappeared. Definitely the best place for a gunman to have shot at Kyle Smith. Good visibility and plenty of cover. Jock's chest tingled as the adrenaline rushed through him. The snow had been disturbed, as if someone had been hiding there, waiting. He did a visual check, snapping a couple of photos with his phone before the snow covered it. No casings. No other evidence he could see.

Three sets of tracks led away from the road—Miller's, Bruce's and the gunman's. Jock followed them around the back of a slightly rundown house that needed a refresh of its light blue painted walls. Snow coated its darker blue roof, and snowdrifts lined the yard. The same spruce trees that lined the back of his mom's place did so here too. There hadn't been enough wind to knock the layers of snow off the tree branches, so they stood caked like Christmas decorations.

Jock cast an eye over the back of the house. Nothing suggested the owner was home. May have even shut the place up for the winter. The three sets of tracks continued, and from the footprints, Jock guessed the shooter had started running once he was out of firing range. Jock picked up the pace, calling in his location to dispatch. "Miller, where are you?"

The officer got back to him right away. "Two houses down from Smith's. The tracks end with a set of tires." One more backyard to go, and he'd be with them.

Jock's heart sank. "I'm right behind you." He jumped the low, snow-covered bushes separating the houses and paused at the sound of a truck backing into the driveway. He climbed back over the bushes and raised his weapon. Walking close to the side of the house, he peered toward the driveway. Not an F-150.

"Miller, I'm approaching a potential witness next door." Witness or attacker.

The ancient, white Chevrolet Silverado truck stopped,

the sound of the handbrake ratcheted, and the driver's door swung open.

Jock stepped toward the door. "Police! Hands in the air!"

An older woman's gloved hands emerged, raised. "Hold your horses!"

Jock held his Glock steady, stepping toward the driver, as Miller and Bruce raced up the driveway. "Place your hands on your head and step out of the vehicle!"

"Is that you, Jock O'Halloran?" Caroline's raised voice was filled with confusion. She peered around the doorframe. "What's the problem?"

Jock lowered his gun, stepping toward his mom's friend. "Sorry about that, Caroline. We were chasing down a suspect."

"You mean that gray F-150 that just barreled down the road like he had a moose on his tail?" Caroline emerged from the truck, shutting the door behind her.

Bruce came and sniffed Caroline, whining.

She patted him on the head. "There boy, are you all excited about something?"

He whined again, and Miller called him to heel.

"Are you sure it was an F-150?" Jock holstered his gun.

"I know my vehicles, son. Could've been the one at your mom's the day of the fire. It had a couple of smashed windows. Looked like they'd been taped." Caroline wiped her hands on her pants.

Jock's neck prickled. There was a high probability the attacker could've changed out the flat tire and patched up the blown-out windows. If only they'd reacted quicker. Could've caught him. If Kyle Smith hadn't been smoking, maybe Bruce would've sniffed out the shooter earlier.

"What are *you* doing here?" Miller's postured stiffened, and his eyes narrowed.

"Just checking on the house for Bob. He's out of town." Caroline pulled a set of house keys out of her jacket pocket. That explained the look of abandonment.

The sirens were coming up the street. Jock reached for his radio and issued a BOLO for the gray F-150, his jaw clenched. Surely someone had seen something.

Phoebe's throat thickened when she learned of Kyle Smith's death. If she hadn't mentioned his messages to Jock, he'd probably still be alive. That was three deaths now. How many more people might be hurt or killed before they solved Ronnie's murder? Someone must be desperate to cover up the truth, and the more destruction that followed her arrival, the more Phoebe worried that it just wasn't worth the fight.

When Jock returned to the station, he'd reassured her that none of this was her fault. But she had a hard time believing it. Thankfully, he seemed happy to have them stay with him at his house. The man made her feel safer than she'd felt since before her dad had left. Ronnie had stoked her insecurities. Making her feel inadequate. Jock did the opposite.

She gathered up a very sleepy Charlie, who'd been filled to the brim with some of Marge's delicious baked goods, and followed Jock out to his vehicle. The sun was long gone, and floodlights illuminated the parking lot. The vehicle had been quickly patched up, and its smashed windows replaced. The chief had signed off on it being fine to drive.

"Kyle Smith gave a statement to Miller and me. We might not be able to call him at trial, but he gave us good information." Jock explained what the man had said as he drove Phoebe and Charlie back to his place. The fact

Jock, Miller and Bruce had been in danger again made her stomach roil.

The modest house was located in town, not far from Cordova PD. Jock mentioned that some friends lived a few doors down—a US marshal and his elementary school teacher wife. They had a daughter the same age as Charlie.

"I have the day off tomorrow. Maybe we could go to church together, if that'd suit you?" Jock asked the question with zero hesitation. That he assumed Phoebe was a churchgoer made her feel both special, and a little fraudulent. Well, she *had* been a churchgoer once. Maybe attending with Jock would help get her back on track with the Lord.

Phoebe smiled. "That'd be great."

A relaxed smile crossed Jock's face.

"Come on, little man. Let's get you ready for bed." She carried Charlie into the bedroom, where someone had set up a cot, toddler sleeping bag, blanket and various thoughtful additions. A little normality for her son wouldn't hurt, and a church service would help. He hadn't been to church more than a handful of times, and if she intended to get back into the habit when she returned to Tucson, this was a good place to start. Besides, some time with other children would do Charlie good too. With Phoebe mostly taking him with her to dance classes, where there were always helping hands, he hadn't spent much time on playdates or other activities with children his own age.

With Charlie settled down for the night, Phoebe walked back out to the living room, where Jock had Ronnie's case file laid out on the coffee table. "Do you ever take a break?"

Jock looked up, swallowing. "I don't usually bring files home. But I wanted to compare what Kyle Smith said to the case file while it's fresh in my mind."

"I appreciate everything you're doing, Jock. It's above

and beyond, especially hosting us at your home." A comfortable warmth filled her.

"It's no big deal. You're safer here than anywhere else. I doubt the attacker will try anything tonight. With patrols searching for his vehicle, he'd be a fool to come into town now." He gave her a slight smile. "You must be exhausted. Why don't you get some rest?"

Phoebe stretched her arms over her head. "I'm still a little wired from the shootout. When the sirens went off again, I think my adrenaline spiked even more."

"Okay, then take a seat, at least." He patted the dark beige sofa near him, closing up the file. "Can I get you anything?"

"No, thanks." Phoebe sank into the comfortable, oversize cushions. Her gaze landed on Ronnie's file. It had expanded since she first saw it, now that Jock had printed out photos and other case notes.

"We'll get to the bottom of it." Jock's voice softened, drawing Phoebe's eyes to him. He'd changed out of his uniform into jeans and a sweater, and the low light of the lamp brought out the slight strawberry tint in his hair. A five o'clock shadow covered his normally clean-shaven jaw. "I'm not the only one following up leads."

"I know." She leaned against the arm of the sofa, curling her feet under her. "I wish I knew why these people want me dead. Do they think you'll stop investigating if I die? It doesn't make sense." She ran her fingers through her hair, propping her head up.

Jock shook his head. "Maybe they think you know something." He focused his gaze on her. "Is there anything you might have left out? Maybe you thought it was irrelevant."

Phoebe frowned. "I honestly can't think of anything else. Kyle's messages would fall into that category, but you know about that now." She brought her hand to her lips. "Do you think Ronnie might have been into something criminal? Did you check his bank statements?"

Jock nodded. "Like you said, nothing out of the ordinary. Unless he had another bank account?"

"You mean one he didn't share with me?" Phoebe's cheeks burned.

"It's not uncommon, and it's not your fault." Jock's brow creased with sincerity.

Phoebe shook her head. "I was his wife. Surely I should've known whether he had a secret bank account, or whatever else he might have been up to..." Tears burned her eyes, and she blinked them back.

Jock reached over to snag her hand. "I'm not saying it to make you feel better. People are good at hiding things. That's one of the reasons I have a job." The steadiness of him sent a wave of warmth through her. *Maybe he has a point.*

Phoebe grinned. "Is that why you became a police officer? To dig into other people's secrets?"

"No, but it's a perk." Jock winked, then let go of her hand with a squeeze. "My father was a police officer, right here in Cordova. I don't remember much about him, so I wanted to feel a little closer. Doing the same job seemed..." He paused, giving a slight grimace. "I guess, it just seemed right."

Phoebe's heartbeat slowed. "I didn't realize that he was a police officer. When your mom said he died at work... was he killed in the line of duty?"

"Yeah." He gave a heavy sigh.

"Wow, I can see why that would've been hard for your mom." Phoebe imagined she'd feel less than delighted if Charlie decided to become a fisherman.

"Yep. She wasn't impressed when I pointed out I could be hit by a car or die of a heart attack if I were an accountant or something *safer*." He sighed. "Not my most sensitive moment."

Phoebe stifled a grin. "Hopefully, she can appreciate you're great at your job, and that you enjoy it."

He paused, as if she'd said something unexpected. "That's kind of you to say." The wistful look in his eye suggested there was more to the story.

I'll have to work out what.

The next morning, they arrived at Cordova Community Church just before ten. Members of the congregation hurried from the parking lot toward the church, bundled in coats and snow boots against the steadily falling flakes of snow.

Music and chatter flowed toward them as they stepped into the foyer, along with smell of freshly brewed coffee. Two obviously pregnant women, a blonde and a brunette, broke away from a group, rushing to greet Phoebe.

"Phoebe Tait! I'm Rachel Miller, you've met my husband, Sam." The enthusiasm of the brunette set her instantly at ease.

"Yes, of course, Officer Miller." Phoebe returned her smile.

Jock smiled at the other woman. "And this is Beth Cruz, the neighbor I mentioned."

"Good to meet you." Phoebe tried to settle Charlie, who wriggled in her arms.

Beth smiled. "We're so happy you came today, especially you, Charlie." She gave Charlie an extra big smile, and the toddler hid his face behind Mr. Snuffles, grinning. "We've been looking forward to meeting you."

Phoebe's breath bottled in her chest. She'd never been welcomed like this before.

Officer Miller and a Hispanic man who also had a law enforcement vibe approached, each shaking Jock's hand.

Beth gave the man a kiss on the cheek. "This is my husband, Jake." Must be the US marshal Jock had mentioned.

Jake gave Phoebe a quick smile. "The service is starting soon."

Rachel gestured toward the doors to the chapel. "Why don't you come in and find a comfy seat? Katie's been keeping an eye on the little ones."

Jock hung back with the men while Phoebe followed the women through the pews and toward the front row—much closer to the action than she'd expected. A girl with loose blond ringlets who Phoebe guessed must be Katie, around nine or ten years old, sat next to two younger girls—one Charlie's age, and the other around three years old.

Charlie peered toward them with interest, and Phoebe popped him on the ground, where he clung to her leg.

Rachel pointed to the older girl. "This is Katie, and my other daughter, Valentina. And the youngest is Marina, Jake and Beth's daughter." Must be the one Jock had mentioned.

After more introductions, Rachel leaned against the pew. "Jock said you have a dance studio in Tucson?"

Phoebe blushed. "Well, I own it with my friend. We teach dance classes for all ages, but I focus on the younger groups."

Beth piped up. "You know, if you get sick of the desert, you're welcome here. We need a dance studio in Cordova. The girls love dancing, and there are so many moms I know who would enroll their daughters."

Phoebe's breath caught in her chest. Move to Cordova?

That wasn't going to happen. She opened her mouth to say so when Rachel leaned forward.

"And sons." Rachel's comment made Beth gasp.

"You decided to find out?"

Rachel nodded, smiling. "Dr. Jackson told us on Friday."

"Congratulations," Phoebe said, and Rachel smiled her thanks.

"I'm sure Samuel's excited there's finally another male in the house." Beth patted her bump. "I know Jake's not-so-secretly hopeful for one of his own. He's pretty keen to take him out kayaking and fishing."

Phoebe bowed her head. Charlie wouldn't have a father to teach him to fish. Even if Ronnie hadn't been the perfect husband, he was an okay dad.

"I'm so sorry." Beth blushed. "I didn't think."

Rachel gave Phoebe a pat on the arm. "Charlie seems to be doing great. I want to hear more about your dance school. What age do they start?"

How did Rachel sense that Phoebe didn't particularly want their sympathy? Whatever the reason, she was grateful.

She forced a smile. "Usually three or four years old, but it depends on what styles. At our studio, we have toddler classes, which are more focused on rhythm, music and movement."

Rachel clapped her hands. "That sounds great! I seriously wish we had that here. Katie is always twirling around the house with Valentina."

Phoebe allowed herself to imagine for a moment what it would be like to live in a welcoming community like this where she'd see her students at church and maybe help choreograph the Christmas pageant. *Don't be silly; you're only here temporarily.* For Ronnie. Besides, she couldn't let Keziah down.

Moments later, Jock slipped in beside her as the service leader stepped to the lectern.

After a short greeting and some community notices, the service began with familiar modern hymns. Phoebe sang along until they were asked to be seated. How she'd missed this. Though they'd married in a church, and Ronnie had outwardly professed to be a Christian, he'd mocked her faith so much she'd felt foolish for believing in the Lord, let alone attending church. Now it was too late to recover the years she'd spent turning her back on the Lord. Too late to return to the faith she'd had as a child.

The children and Beth left for Sunday school, including Charlie, who'd gravitated toward the girls and was playing with a toy that Marina had shared with him.

A middle-aged man with light brown, slightly thinning hair and reading glasses stood at the front. He had a friendly face and smiled at the congregation while he adjusted his over-ear microphone.

"Can you think of a time you lost something so precious that you'd drop everything and go search for it until you got it back?" He paused.

A few yeps and grunts of affirmation. Phoebe's mind returned to the moment she'd turned to see Charlie gone. Her skin prickled, and she tried to swallow down the emotion that threatened to spill over.

"It's not a great feeling, is it?" Phoebe tried to put aside the memory of Charlie and focus on the message.

"One day, in the middle of New York City, my youngest son, Josiah, ran off in a crowd, and I couldn't find him." The pastor raised his hands in defeat. "He'd promised me that he'd stay close by, so you can imagine my surprise…" The congregation chuckled.

"It took an hour to track him down. The longest hour of my life." Some murmurs of sympathy came from the congregation, and Phoebe's throat ached as she gave an understanding nod. How fresh that feeling was for her.

"You can only imagine my relief when he came back. I kissed that kid so hard, he didn't know what'd hit him. The lost child had been found!" He glanced around the congregation. "His disobedience was the *last* thing on my mind." His eyes momentarily paused on Phoebe. "That's how the Lord feels when *you* come back to Him. That's why He sent His only Son—the Son who He loved, who pleased Him. Not to judge, but to rescue the lost. To rescue *you*." His gaze left Phoebe, and he continued. "Now let's turn to that lost older brother in the parable of the prodigal son—or prodigal *sons* as I prefer to title it."

Phoebe's heart raced. Could that be true? Did the Lord feel her loss as keenly as she'd felt Charlie's? Would the Lord really welcome her back with open arms? Even when she'd abandoned Him to focus on the distractions and things of the world? Seemed too good to be true.

Jock's phone buzzed next to her, and he whispered in her ear. "I need to go. I'll be back soon."

The next hymn started, and Phoebe grabbed his arm as he stood. "Where?"

He hesitated. "The fire department spotted the gray truck."

Phoebe's gut dropped. She glanced over at Marge, the deaths of Ethan Davis and Kyle Smith playing on her mind. If Jock was headed out, no way she'd let him go on his own.

"I'm coming with you."

SIX

Phoebe tried to look as certain as possible. Jock *had* to say yes.

He gave her a small smile. "No need, it's been abandoned. I want to cordon off the area before anyone contaminates the scene. Won't take long."

Miller leaned in from behind. "What's going on?"

Jock filled him in. "Pete Morrow saw it parked at the end of Eyak Lake Highway while he was checking a rockslide at Power Creek. The fire department had a call out that someone was trapped. It was a false alarm."

"If it's abandoned, let Garrison and Hunt do it. They're on shift." Miller gave Rachel a slight shrug in answer to her pointed stare.

"They're dealing with some domestic disturbance. This isn't a priority." He glanced at Phoebe. It *was* for her.

Miller drew a deep breath. "I'll come with you."

"You've got that lunch. It's fine. I can go alone." Jock patted him on the shoulder.

Phoebe's heart raced. *He's doing this for my sake. I can't let him go alone.* "I told you, I'm coming with you." No way would she let Jock go alone in this weather. Not when the situation was of *her* making. Charlie must have settled into Sunday school, since Beth hadn't come to get her. He'd be okay without her for a half hour or so. Besides, Marge was there. Between the moms and grandmas, not to mention a US marshal and police officer, he'd be safe. She swallowed. "Didn't the chief tell you not to leave my side?"

Miller shook his head. "I don't think Chief Anderson will sign off on you going."

"I'm not staying here." Phoebe set her jaw, and a few parishioners began to stare.

Jock sighed, speaking to Miller. "I'll talk to the chief. Let my mom know, would you?" The hymn finished, and Jock grabbed Phoebe's hand as everyone took their seats.

They walked toward the doors, and Jock dialed. She tuned out as he filled the chief in, her mind returning to the pastor's sermon. She sure needed the Lord now. They all did. *Lord, will You really welcome me back? Will You listen to my prayers?*

"He doesn't want me to leave your side." Jock pressed his lips together. "You don't have to do this. It'd be better for you to stay here."

Phoebe shook her head. "I told you, I'm coming. The chief agrees."

Jock cleared his throat then helped Phoebe into her coat. "I guess there might be something in the truck that gives us a clue who's after you. You can have a look inside. That'd be worth the trip." They headed out the door into the parking lot.

Ten minutes later, they rounded Eyak Lake, its frozen expanse stretching alongside them, before their vehicle climbed away from the lake, following Power Creek into the forest to the trailhead. Snow blew toward them in lazy flakes, blotting out the weak sunlight. The fire truck had been through in the early hours, making a path, but Jock drove slowly as they ascended.

"Wonder why he'd be this far past the lake." Jock glanced at Phoebe. "It's a strange place to leave it unless he had a buddy to pick him up. Those trails lead to nowhere." He cleared his throat. "Maybe that's why. If the fire department hadn't been called out, it might've been lost for months."

Phoebe's stomach quivered. The narrow road was slippery, and it seemed like they were in the middle of nowhere. "Where did they see it?"

Jock rolled slowly past a house that had been boarded up for the winter. "He said it's parked near the trailhead. We should be able to drive right up to it since the fire truck made it."

Moments later, the gray truck came into view. It sat abandoned, just as the fire chief had described.

They pulled up alongside it, and Jock wound down his window, peering into the cab. "There's a duffel bag in the front seat." He reached for his sidearm. "You should stay here while I check it out." He left the engine running, the heater continuing to blast warm air into the cab.

Phoebe's mouth dried. "You said you'd just be cordoning it off. Why do you need your gun?" *Lord, if You're listening, please protect us.*

"It's just a precaution. Maybe duck down, just in case." He reached for his radio. "Dispatch, we've located the vehicle."

"Copy that, O'Halloran."

Jock leaned forward, when *Bang!* A rifle round smashed through the window, narrowly missing his head. Jock grabbed Phoebe's shoulder, shoving her down below the window.

Her ears rang from the shot. Another round fired, hitting the doorframe. Phoebe's heart raced, and she peered over the dash. They'd been lured into a trap!

“Stay down.” Jock backed the vehicle up until the gray truck was between them and the shooter. “Shots fired at police!”

What had she been thinking, coming out here? So much for a routine cordoning off of an abandoned vehicle. Now Jock was in even more danger!

A man came running toward them, sliding to a rest next to Phoebe’s door. “Let me in!”

Phoebe gasped, shrinking back toward Jock. He’d already wound down her window, leaning over Phoebe to shove his gun in the man’s face. “Hands in the air!”

The man complied, and Jock kept his weapon and eyes trained on him.

“Don’t move!” He tossed the man some handcuffs. “Cuff yourself.”

The man complied, eyeing Jock’s gun. “We need to go! Now!”

Phoebe’s hands quivered with adrenaline as she took in the sunken eyes. The brown buzz cut. This was the man who’d tried to kill her. Who’d snatched Charlie! “Jock… It’s him.”

Another rifle round rang out, shooting through the glass of the gray truck and slamming into Jock’s seat. If he hadn’t moved, he’d be hit! *Thank You, Lord.*

The man ducked down below the window, and Phoebe whispered, “Aren’t you going to arrest him?”

Jock glanced toward the slope from where the bullet had come. “My priority is keeping you safe.”

Phoebe swallowed. “Whatever he knows about Ronnie’s death will die with him if we don’t bring him with us.”

“I know.” Jock gave her arm a squeeze. “Don’t worry.” He flung open the back door and yelled at the man. “Get in!”

The man climbed in, awkwardly sliding into the back

seat. He shivered, his face red from the cold. How long had he been out there? And why?

Jock took out some cable ties and fastened his cuffs to the vehicle. "Who's shooting at us?"

The man didn't respond.

Another round fired, this time missing Phoebe by an inch. She flinched. "We need to go!" The questions could wait.

Jock clipped himself back in, then put his foot down, skidding out from behind the cover of the gray truck and onto the road. A bullet hit the back of the vehicle, and the impact swayed them slightly toward the edge of the road. Jock brought them back. Hopefully once they got into the trees, the shooter wouldn't have a clean shot.

"What's your name?" Jock's aggressive tone shocked Phoebe, but she understood. He needed the man to answer. They both did.

The man shook his head.

"I can dump you out right here. You can take your chances with the shooter or freeze to death. You were half-way there already!"

"Beau Thomas," the man hissed through gritted teeth.

Jock navigated the terrain, his jaw set. "*Beau* sounds a lot like *Moe* or *Joe*, doesn't it?" He didn't need to share a look with Phoebe to help her connect the dots. Kyle Smith's pre-death testimony was confirmed.

Just as Phoebe thought they'd managed to get away safely, headlights flared behind them, and Jock grunted. "That was quick."

Phoebe turned to look, holding up her hand to shield her eyes from the high beams. No way could they identify the vehicle or the driver with that brightness. "He can't shoot us while he's driving."

Jock set his jaw, pressing his foot on the accelerator. The vehicle leaped forward, hugging the road as they retraced the path they'd made earlier. Snow-covered spruce trees and scrubby bushes climbed the slope to one side. To the other, the sheer drop sent a chill down Phoebe's spine. If they went over the edge… Didn't bear thinking about.

Moments later, the vehicle ran into the back of them. On the unplowed, slippery road, their vehicle weaved to the left.

Phoebe gasped, gripping the door handle.

"Whoa!" Jock gripped the steering wheel, returning the vehicle to the middle of the road as he reached for the radio. His jaw clenched, and he sped up, giving their location to the dispatcher. "I can't identify the vehicle. It's an SUV or a truck, but I can't see a color, model or make in these conditions."

The dispatcher replied, "I have a unit twenty minutes out."

Their pursuer rammed them again, this time on a corner. The police vehicle slid on the ice, toward the edge.

Phoebe's adrenaline spiked. Could Jock get them out of this?

The tires continued to slide, and Jock's brow furrowed in concentration. Then the vehicle bumped them again, and he set his jaw. "Hold on, we're going over."

His terrifyingly calm voice sent a spike of dread through Phoebe's gut. Would they end up in the water? She grasped the handle, trying to press her body into the seat.

Beau Thomas exclaimed as the vehicle teetered on the edge before the momentum sent them over.

The screech of metal, smash of shattering glass and thud of Jock's head against the steering wheel made Phoebe's teeth rattle. Her limbs flailed as she was tossed like a boat in a swell, with only the seat belt holding her in place. Her left arm caught on the gearshift, wrenching at an unnatural angle until she screamed with pain. A pile of snow crashed through the gaping window and into her face, peaking her adrenaline.

After what felt like forever, the vehicle came to a shuddering halt, wedged against something immovable. Steam spilled into the cab, along with the smell of diesel. Phoebe's cheeks burned, and her arm throbbed. She tried to turn to check on Jock, but the movement of her arm made her howl. Moving her good arm, her right arm, thankfully, she gingerly felt around until she could touch the left. It'd been caught at an odd angle, and she needed to move it if she was going to get out of this mess. Drawing a deep breath and pressing her lips together, she eased it back in front of her with a gasp, then gently turned toward Jock. He was out cold, a large gash on his forehead. Would anyone find them? *I need to call for help.*

A groaning, grunting sound came from the back. Beau Thomas was obviously alive. Well, he could stay in the back.

She reached over for Jock's radio, breathing through the pain, and pressed the button as she'd seen him do. "Help! We need help!"

The dispatcher came online. "What is your location?"

"I don't know, wherever Jock—Officer O'Halloran—said. He's unconscious. I'm injured." A bullet slammed into the cab, and Phoebe whimpered. "And someone's shooting at us!"

"Hang in there, help is on the way." The calmness of the dispatcher's voice did little to reassure Phoebe.

Lord, if You don't want us to die, You'll have to do something.

She caught sight of Jock's gun in its holster. If she could just reach it, maybe she could shoot back. At least hold the attacker at bay until help came.

Another shot rang out, this time ricocheting off the window frame. *Too close*. She had to get that gun, now, no matter how painful. She pressed her injured arm against her chest and reached toward Jock. *Bang!* The bullet embedded where her head had been. *They can see us!* She grabbed the gun, pointed it in the direction from where the bullet had come, and fired.

The dispatcher's voice came through. "Are you with me, Mrs. Tait?"

Phoebe didn't answer, firing again. No way would backup arrive in time to help. How were they going to get out of this mess?

Jock opened his eyes to a bright light, disoriented. "O'Halloran, can you hear me?" He recognized the deep voice of Chief Anderson. "His eyes are open, but he's not responding. Can't you get him out faster?"

The sound of heavy machinery nearby hurt his ears. *Where am I?* The pain in his head made him squint then close his eyes.

"O'Halloran, stay with me! Get that gurney!" The chief's voice faded.

The next time Jock opened his eyes, the chief's voice had been replaced by a woman's. She spoke in hushed tones. He blinked, trying to focus his eyes, and the distinctive swish of a hospital curtain being closed brought him back into the room. The harsh hospital lighting drilled into his retinas, and he closed them again.

What did he last remember? Phoebe had been next to him. They'd been in the car with the detainee. Someone had run into them. They'd gone over the edge; the vehicle had tipped, and…that was all. *Must've blacked out.* He reached for his head. Was that a bandage? *Must've banged my head.* Did he sustain any other injuries? He blinked again, and his eyes focused. Limbs okay. Full range of movement.

Phoebe. His heart rate ticked up. Had she made it out of the car wreck alive? *Lord, I couldn't stand it if she's…*

Before he could think any further, a loud grunt of dissatisfaction sounded.

"Mr. Thomas, I don't have a key. The officer will be able to help you when he returns." A stern woman's voice—maybe a nurse—came through the whisper-thin curtain separating him from the other patient. Thomas? This wasn't a large place. Must be Beau Thomas. He remembered that too. The man had somehow managed to reappear in an abandoned vehicle at the end of a dead-end road. Didn't make sense. Hopefully he'd get a chance to talk to him. His eyes shot open—this time the light wasn't so painful.

Thomas gave a disgusted grunt, and the nurse said, "There's no need for that."

She pulled aside the curtain and smiled. Jock caught a glimpse of Thomas's scowl before the nurse drew the curtain and snagged the clipboard from the end of his bed. Her salt-and-pepper hair had been pulled back in a neat bun, and her pressed blue uniform matched her glasses. She clicked a pen and wrote something on the record.

"Officer O'Halloran, glad to see you're awake." Her voice had lost its sternness, was instead filled with sympathy. "You got a nasty cut on your head and a concussion, so we're keeping you here until we've done the CT scan." That explained the bandage.

"What about Phoebe—Mrs. Tait?" If Jock only had a concussion, hopefully Phoebe hadn't come off much worse.

But why wasn't she in the adjoining bed? A sick feeling rose in his stomach. What if something had happened to her? His heart lurched, and he realized she meant more to him than he'd anticipated. He didn't mean to feel this way. Couldn't. Not with his family history.

"You know I'm bound by HIPAA." She leaned toward him and winked. "But just between us, she's had surgery to repair a broken ulna, otherwise fine. She's in recovery."

The whiplash of relief left him with a sudden lightheadedness. "Thanks, I appreciate that." A broken forearm wasn't the end of the world. *Thank You, Lord, for keeping her safe.*

The nurse took his vitals, writing them on the clipboard as she went. She slipped it back into the console at the end of the bed, plumped his pillow and patted him on the shoulder. "You rest up now, and I'll be back in an hour to check on you."

"Thanks."

She left, swishing the curtain back into place.

Jock leaned back into the pillow. A concussion, huh? How long had he been out? Didn't think to ask after the detainee, but maybe the chief could fill him in. What had happened? Had they caught the driver that'd run them off the road? Could he in some way be related to Beau Thomas? What about Charlie? Jock needed to call his mom, check if they'd made it safely home from church. *Where's my phone?*

Thankfully, someone must've retrieved it from his pocket, as it lay on the table next to the bed. He leaned over to grab it, and his head spun. Grabbing the side table, he tried to steady himself. Only, the lock must've been disengaged because it rolled away, pivoting through the curtain and coming to rest with a crash against the adjacent bed. Still gripping the table, he waited for the dizziness to abate. The curtain had opened, and Beau Thomas sat propped in bed, staring at him. In place of the scowl he'd offered the nurse, his expression appeared subdued. His face had been cut up a bit, and he had a large bruise on his left cheekbone. An officer must've cuffed his wrist to the metal bedrail, and he'd kicked off the sheets. Beneath his expressionless face, Jock sensed the man's fear. Maybe this presented Jock with an opportunity to get him to talk.

Leaving his phone for the moment, Jock locked the wheels on the table and leaned against it. "How are you doing?"

"Someone just tried to kill me. How d'you think I'm doing?" Thomas glowered at him.

Jock tilted his head to the side. "Why do they want you dead?"

The man snorted. "They want to keep me quiet."

Jock considered this for a moment. Why hadn't the shooter come and finished the job? With Jock incapacitated, he could've shot Beau Thomas in the car wreck. Maybe Phoebe could shed some light on it if she'd managed to stay conscious throughout the ordeal. Jock winced at the thought of her lying in pain, waiting for help. Whoever had tried to kill them needed to be held accountable.

"Who's *they*?" Jock's nostrils flared.

"Nope, you're not getting anything else. Not until I get a deal. Give me immunity from prosecution, and you'll get everything I know." Thomas sneered.

Jock considered the man's proposition. If he had something useful, it sure would be handy to have more information. But in the unlikely event a deal might be offered, the district attorney was the only one with the authority to make it. Still, Thomas didn't know his chances were near zero. "That's not how it works, Mr. Thomas. Do you have a lawyer?"

The man shrugged. "I don't like lawyers."

"You'd be wise to get one. They can negotiate the deal. But while we're here, is there anything you can tell me that I can take to the DA? He's the one who'd be negotiating with you or your lawyer. I doubt you'll be at the top of his priority list if I don't have something to offer." Beau Thomas frowned, and opened his mouth to speak, but Jock held up his hand. The frown wasn't one of thoughtful cooperation. Better to let him stew a bit. "Don't decide now. You think about what I've said and let me know before I leave. Things always go better for those who cooperate." That ought to give the man time to come up with something useful. In the meantime, he needed to see Phoebe.

He didn't get far. The nurse caught him walking out of the room and escorted him straight back to bed with a stern rebuke. But he convinced the nurse aide to wheel him into recovery next to Phoebe once he'd had the CT scan.

Her face broke into a weak smile. "You're okay." Phoebe looked tired, her hair disheveled and her eyes bloodshot from the anesthetic. Jock's chest tightened with a mixture of relief and admiration. Phoebe had already been through so much, but she wasn't complaining.

"Yeah, I'm fine. I'm so sorry that you got hurt." Jock blew out a breath. Could've been so much worse.

Phoebe sank back into her pillow. "Yeah. When he opened fire, I didn't think we'd make it."

"Opened fire?" Jock went still.

"Yeah, you hit your head early on and blacked out. Beau Thomas yelled something about not being silenced, and the guy who ran us off the road shot at us. I grabbed your gun and shot back, and that seemed to stop him." Phoebe shifted in the bed. "He left pretty quickly, and then the cavalry showed up."

Jock's stomach knotted. They'd missed this other attacker. Where did this individual fit into Ronnie's case? "Did Beau Thomas say anything useful?"

"He might've done, but to be honest, I was in too much pain to hear him." She ran her unbandaged hand through her hair. "I'm okay now, thanks to the analgesics." Jock's heart lurched at the thought of Phoebe in pain.

Before Jock could ask more questions, his mom arrived, followed by Chief Anderson.

Marge's face appeared pale, and her eyes wide. "What on earth were you thinking?"

Jock wasn't sure at whom she'd directed the question. He swallowed, waiting for her to clarify.

"You both could've been killed!" Marge looked between Phoebe and Jock, then gave Chief Anderson a glare.

The chief gave Jock a look that said *let's talk.* Wasn't a suggestion. He walked out into the passageway, and Jock licked his lips. "Give me a moment."

His mom shook her head then sat in the chair next to Phoebe's bed with a heavy sigh. "Charlie's absolutely fine. Delightful. He and Marina are as thick as thieves."

Jock walked from the room, leaving the wheelchair behind, and sat next to the chief on one of the visitors' chairs. There were few visitors. A young couple spoke in low voices with a doctor. The smell of fresh coffee wafted toward them.

"How're you holding up, O'Halloran?"

"I'm fine, Chief. They're keeping me in overnight as a precaution, but if all is well, I'll be back on deck next shift." Jock went to run his hand through his hair, but the bandage stopped him. He lowered his hand into his lap.

Chief Anderson nodded. "Good. What's Beau Thomas said so far?"

Jock filled him in. "Not much. All we know for sure is that he's stalked Phoebe, broken into her house and tried to kidnap her son. I'm convinced he's got something to do with Ronnie Tait's death. At the very least he knows who's responsible. I'll humor him and talk to the DA's office, but I don't think he'll give me much. Thomas believes the other shooter wants to kill him. I'll do my best to make him see we're his best option if he wants to stay alive."

"You do that, and I'll call the DA. He can sort out the charges." The chief looked around then said, "You did *not* tell me you planned to take Mrs. Tait with you to make an arrest. You said, and I quote, 'You don't want me to leave Mrs. Tait out of my sight, do you, Chief?'" He gave Jock a pointed look. "Consider this a first and final warning. Do not pull anything like that again, or I will suspend you. Without pay. Do you understand?"

Jock's stomach dropped. "Yes, sir." If he'd thought Phoebe would be in any danger, he'd never have agreed to take her. His main concern *had* been for her safety. She'd had her heart set on making herself useful, and he figured it was a battle he didn't need to pick. *Thank You, Lord, that my foolishness didn't end her life.* He'd listen to his gut in the future.

"The only reason you're still on the job is because I think you've suffered enough." The chief clapped him on the arm, giving him a squeeze. "Now, get yourself some rest."

They parted ways, and Jock returned to his room, where Beau Thomas ate dinner with the hand that wasn't cuffed to the bed. He gave Jock a reproachful look, then fixed his eyes on his plate.

Jock's own dinner languished on the side table. No use

letting it go to waste. He opened the dividing curtain and sat on the bed. "You had a chance to think about things?"

He took a bite of the chicken breast, regarding the broccoli and mashed potatoes with skepticism. The chicken didn't hold a candle to his mom's.

Beau Thomas looked up from his meal. "Yeah." He gave Jock a pointed look. "Lawyer. That's all I'm saying until I get a deal."

Jock's chest tightened. All that the thinking time had done was convince him to lawyer up. "That's not enough. Think harder. Depending on what the hospital says, we'll interview you tomorrow."

"Don't leave it too long." Thomas lowered his voice. "Or he'll come back and finish the job."

"We can protect you. But you need to give me something more than a no-comment interview."

Thomas shrugged, turning away with a dismissive grunt.

Unease lifted the hair on the back of Jock's neck. Phoebe was in even more danger than he'd known, and the only person who could help identify the threat wasn't talking. *Lord, I'll do what I can, but I need Your help.* What if Thomas was right about his days being numbered? If they could get to Thomas, they could get to Phoebe. He clenched his fists. No way could he allow that to happen.

SEVEN

How Phoebe longed to hold Charlie again. Marge had assured her that he was safe and happy, but her heart ached to see him. Last night, Marge had left him with Beth and Jake for the night, which put Phoebe's mind at ease. A schoolteacher and US marshal could keep him happy and safe. Though Marge had gone home to sleep, she'd promised to be back this morning. Poor Marge. How stressful it must have been for her to receive the call that Jock had been in a car wreck. All of the memories from her husband's death would've come flooding back. *He wouldn't be in hospital if I'd stayed in Tucson.* Didn't help that her own mom had left a tetchy voicemail chastising her for leaving home without redirecting her mail. Apparently, it had caused her a *lot* of inconvenience. No questions about Phoebe or Charlie's well-being. Phoebe drew a deep breath. She'd have to call her mom back sometime, but it probably wouldn't be today.

Hopefully, she'd be discharged shortly. Her phone pinged, and an unknown number appeared.

Next time there won't be survivors. Leave town now.

The message made her blood run cold, and her chest tightened with guilt. Now, no doubt remained that Jock had been injured because of her. Her hands shook, and her breath hitched. The message couldn't have been from Beau Thomas—he remained cuffed to his hospital bed, with zero technology allowed. Must be from the person with the rifle. A heaviness overcame her, and tears pricked her eyes.

"Phoebe, are you okay?" Jock's voice startled her, and she glanced up. The unexpected relief she'd felt when she saw him for the first time since the accident had made her heart lurch. It did the same again now. *He's okay.* This time, he'd changed back into his uniform, and the only indication something had happened was the medical dressing on his head. That meant the hospital was happy with his progress. *Must've discharged him.* Until now, she'd been focused on her guilt about getting him hurt, not any feelings she had for the man. But this sense of relief? Surely, she'd be just as relieved for any other officer. Wouldn't she?

"I'm okay. It's just the thought of what might've happened." Phoebe sniffed back her tears.

Jock sat in the chair Marge had occupied yesterday and reached for her good hand. His touch was reassuring, his fingers warm. "I understand. I'm sorry I put you in that situation. Truly." The remorse on his face caused a flutter of guilt to rush through her. He couldn't take this on himself.

She shook her head. "No, I insisted on coming. I'm the one who should be sorry. Surely, they wouldn't have shot you if you were alone. It's me they want."

His features softened. "I'll find them. I'll get Beau Thomas to talk."

A nurse opened the door, peering toward her with concern. "How are you doing in there?"

"Ready to go home… I mean, get discharged." Phoebe's slip of the tongue made her realize that she didn't hate the idea of this town being home. Which was ridiculous. There was nothing for her here. The dance studio was back in Tucson. Her house was there too. Her best friend, Keziah.

"We have to wait for the doctor. I'll see what she's up to." The nurse smiled and left.

Jock gave her an expectant look, and she realized she had to show him the message.

"Look at this." She took her hand back, reaching for her phone. She missed the warmth of his hand.

He studied the message, shaking his head. "Do you recognize the number?"

Phoebe shuddered. "No, and I don't like that they have mine." The horrible thought that the person knew her number—her unlisted number—made her sick. But maybe someone who knew their way around technology wouldn't have difficulty finding her number. After all, they'd tracked her down to the airport, found where she was staying and managed to catch Officer Miller and Jock off guard with Kyle Smith. If it was the same person behind all of it. *Ronnie, what did you get yourself into?*

Phoebe bowed her head, ashamed that she'd not yet apologized. "I'm so sorry for all the trouble I'm causing. I've been thinking for a while that if I leave, the attacks will stop. If I get the next flight out, maybe things will settle down." Although the thought of leaving Jock behind left her unexpectedly flat. She had to stop any irrational fantasies about this hypothetical life. Home was in Tucson, and Jock should be no concern of hers. Her focus should be on how she was supposed to change diapers and bathe her son with one arm in a cast. *You'll just have to manage.* Like she always had. She thought of her mom's nonexistent offer of help and distinct absence since Ronnie's death and held back a sigh. Maybe not her mom. But Keziah would be there for her. And the kind dance moms who had already given her so much support. Plenty of two-year-olds were potty-trained. Maybe now was a good time to start.

Jock frowned. "Do you really think that leaving would stop them? Beau Thomas already tracked you to your home in Tucson. It'll be much easier to pick you off when you have no protection. I'm sure that's why this person wants you to leave."

Tears welled in Phoebe's eyes at the thought of Charlie being kidnapped again. But she blinked them back, focusing her gaze on the foot of the bed. "Maybe you're right. But how can I stay here and put everyone else in danger?"

Jock retrieved her hand. "If you give up now, Ronnie, Ethan and Kyle have died for one reason only—to hide some unknown and possibly ongoing criminal activity. Is that really what you want?" His tone was filled with compassion, not judgment.

Phoebe shrugged, her limbs heavy. "I guess not."

"I can understand how you'd want to take Charlie home. It's hard here without your friends and family. Your parents must miss you both." Jock gave her hand a squeeze.

"My mom is the only parent left, and I don't think she misses us at all." Phoebe barely kept the bitterness from her voice.

Jock's brow furrowed with concern. "I'm sorry, I didn't know. What makes you think your mom feels that way?"

Something, maybe the warmth in his gaze or the security of her hand in his, made her want to open up to him. "The communication since we've been gone. Look, it's nothing new. I may have had a father for longer than you, but after my parents divorced, I never saw him. He died when I turned fifteen, so I don't much remember what he was like. Mom won custody, which I think in hindsight must've been more to spite Dad than because she wanted to raise me. It became obvious during my tweens that she resented me. The time and financial burden. Every moment and dollar she had to spend on me was one she couldn't spend on herself. I don't want to become like her."

Jock gave his head a slight shake in confusion. "Do you really think you'd become like her? You don't seem like the sort of person who'd have a problem putting others first."

"I don't know. Who knows how jaded and exhausted I might become after ten, fifteen years raising Charlie alone?" She sighed. "I hope I won't. But sometimes I feel so…lost." Using the word *lost* brought back that sermon at the church earlier. Could she rely on the Lord again? Had He been listening to her prayers?

"I understand. A little." Jock's mouth pinched as his expression soured. "At least she didn't remarry."

Phoebe sensed something had changed in Jock. A melancholy seemed to weigh on him. "It sounds like you have some experience. Did your mom remarry?"

Jock's jaw stiffened. "Yep. She was married for ten years—shortly after she lost Dad. I'd just turned twelve when she finally kicked him out." His shoulders slumped. "I wish she'd done it ten years earlier. Would've saved us all a lot of heartache."

Poor Jock. Phoebe hungered to know the details. "Do you mind me asking what happened?"

"There's not much to tell." Jock's heart raced, and he took his hand back. He shouldn't have mentioned Dieter. While he'd forgiven the man, did he really want to reveal his worst moments to Phoebe? Part of him did. But the sensible part knew that he needed to be wary. Phoebe's son was the same age he had been when Dieter came into their lives. Knowing how little his stepfather bonded with him—how abusive he'd been—Jock didn't want to go there. Deep down he knew he'd end up behaving the same way. It was inevitable.

His phone buzzed, saving him. Chief Anderson. Beau Thomas had been discharged from hospital just after Jock. He was on his way to a jail cell in anticipation of his arraignment tomorrow morning.

"Is everything okay?" Phoebe lowered her voice.

"Just a message about Beau Thomas. He'll be arraigned tomorrow morning. I'm hoping I can interview him before that." He replied to his boss's text to that effect, then added the details of the threats on Phoebe's phone. The chief could delegate that.

A knock at the door heralded Marge, who held Charlie. Jock stood, stepping away from the bed to leave room for the little boy.

Charlie gave his mom a huge smile. "Mama! Mama!"

The expression of love on Phoebe's face made Jock's heart contract. How he wished he could keep that little boy safe from whoever Phoebe might bring into his life. No, that wasn't fair. Phoebe wouldn't make a bad decision about that. *Mom did.* It wasn't his business. He needed to let it go. He should focus on protecting mother and child from the current threat, not future hypotheticals. *At least I can protect them from me.*

Marge handed Charlie to Phoebe, carefully nestling the child into the crook of her good arm.

The boy instantly nuzzled into his mom. His bunny was tucked under one arm, and his other hand clutched Phoebe's hospital gown. He spoke to her in words she seemed to understand but were unintelligible to Jock. But the tone said it all. *I love you, Mom, and I missed you so much!*

Phoebe kissed his head, any sign of tears long gone.

Jock's phone buzzed again. His boss requested that he come right in to interview Beau Thomas. Apparently, the man had already arranged a lawyer and was prepared to talk. Jock guessed he wanted to avoid the arraignment by cutting a deal with the DA.

"I have to go into work." Jock straightened his vest, trying not to wince as the action activated both his bruised shoulder and now bruised ribs.

Marge gave him a dubious look. "It's your day off, and you've *just* been discharged."

Phoebe's attention remained on her son, who continued to gaze up at her with adoration.

"I have to interview a witness for Phoebe's case." Jock crossed his arms over his chest.

Phoebe looked up from her son. "Beau Thomas?"

"Yep." He stepped toward the door. "Don't leave until I come back, please."

"Okay." Phoebe nodded, and his mom frowned. About what, Jock didn't have the energy to ask.

Ten minutes later, Officer Miller had picked him up from the hospital, and they were on their way to the interview.

"How did the lunch go, yesterday?" Jock was glad that his friend and colleague was back on shift today. He trusted him to do the interview.

"Uneventful." Miller smiled. "Charlie sure gave Marina a run for her money."

"Did he?" Jock found himself more than casually curious about the little boy.

"Yeah, he's got a real fun personality. Reminds me a little of you." Miller raised his eyebrows.

Jock rolled his eyes. "Are you saying I have the personality of a toddler?"

Miller shrugged, giving him a side eye. "How's Phoebe doing?" Miller slowed at an intersection.

"She's okay. A broken arm and a few bruises." Jock's chin dipped toward his chest. "I should have protected her better."

"Don't beat yourself up. I've been there. When you have a woman you like put her foot down, it's hard to say no." Miller accelerated through the intersection and turned toward the main road.

Jock's cheeks burned. "Who said anything about liking her?"

"Really?" He didn't have to check to know that Miller was raising an eyebrow. "Rachel and Beth were saying you and Phoebe would make a nice couple. They like her."

Great. That was all he needed. Sometimes small-town living really had its downsides. "Phoebe's mourning her husband. Last thing she wants is a relationship. Even if that were on the table. Which, to be clear, it's not."

Miller grunted. "You keep telling yourself that if you want, but I saw the way you looked at her at church yesterday."

Jock's face tingled. "Look, even if I was interested in Phoebe—which I'm not—there's no way I'd do anything about it. I promised myself I'd never be a stepfather. You should know that by now." No point using the excuse of professional boundaries with Miller—he'd met his wife on the job when she'd been in the crosshairs of a psychopathic killer.

Miller took one hand off the wheel and placed it on Jock's shoulder. "Bud, you probably won't listen to me, but I'm going to say it anyway. You are nothing like Dieter. I've seen you with Katie, Valentina, Marina, Paul, not to mention Bruce. Any kid would be blessed to have you as a stepfather. The real question is whether you and Phoebe are meant to be together. If it's what the Lord wants for you, don't stand in the way. Just…pray about it, would you?"

Jock hesitated, unable to come up with a satisfactory reply. Why did he feel so uncertain about this? Why couldn't he dismiss it?

Moments later, they parked and entered the PD. Chief Anderson strode toward them. He locked eyes with Jock. "You ready? The assistant DA's waiting for me in the observation room. Beau Thomas and his attorney are already in the interview room."

"The ADA?" Jock raised his eyebrows.

"Yes, the district attorney's office wants to be involved. Especially when one of our own ends up in hospital, and the guy's about to be arraigned. They want to hear what he has to say." The chief turned and headed to join the ADA.

Miller and Jock walked into the interview room where Beau Thomas and his attorney were seated.

Thomas's sunken eyes had deep shadows beneath them, like he hadn't slept in a week. He looked worse than he had at the hospital, and a slightly sour odor wafted off him. His buzz cut had a few more days of growth, and his slightly hooked nose contrasted with his thin lips. Next to him, the attorney looked like a million bucks. Not a hair out of place and wearing a perfectly laundered charcoal suit. Interesting that Beau Thomas could afford someone beyond the court appointed attorney, and that he could arrange it so quickly. Could he cut a deal with the DA? Jock's stomach tightened. While he was eager to get to the bottom of Ronnie Tait's death, no way did he want Beau Thomas walking away from what he'd done.

"Thanks for coming in, Mr. Thomas." Miller's slow, calm voice went through the mandated procedural comments before he sat back in his chair. "Tell us about Ronnie Tait's death. Were you there when he died?"

"Yes." Beau Thomas didn't elaborate, but Miller waited. It was a tactic Jock had seen him use many times. Just sit there and wait patiently for the other guy to fill the silence.

The minutes stretched, and Beau's lawyer shifted in his seat, as if he'd been sitting for too long.

"What happened?" Miller prompted.

Beau Thomas nervously licked his lips. "It was an accident. Everything that happened in the report was exactly as I said."

I don't believe you. The hairs on Jock's neck prickled. Beau Thomas had confirmed what Jock suspected when he'd spoken with Captain Kemp. There was a lot more to Ronnie Tait's death than met the eye. He glanced at Miller, who nodded, allowing him to ask his own question.

"Mr. Thomas, you've been charged with a list of class A felonies, including attempted homicide and kidnapping. Plus a host of class B and C felonies and misdemeanors, including stalking and reckless endangerment. You told me that you wanted a deal, but you've given us absolutely nothing we don't know." Jock held up his hands. "Are we wasting our time?"

Beau Thomas glanced at his attorney, who leaned and whispered something in his client's ear. Thomas nodded.

The attorney spoke up. "*If* my client committed any crimes, he did so under duress. You were there to witness his life in immediate danger."

Jock wanted to pound his fist against the table. The affirmative defense of duress would allow Beau Thomas to walk away. Thomas hadn't known that when he'd asked for a deal. Maybe he didn't need a deal after all. "Then why are we here?"

"My client is simply asking for protection. He wants to cooperate." The attorney folded his hands on the table. "So long as it doesn't cost him his life."

Miller paused the interview. "We'll need to talk to the district attorney."

The attorney glanced pointedly at the one-way glass behind Jock and Miller. "Please, go ahead and do that."

Jock followed Miller out of the room, closing the door behind them. Something played on his mind. "What do you think he's hiding? What's worth killing over? It can't just be Ronnie Tait's murder."

Miller nodded. "I was thinking the same thing. You know the case better than anyone by now. What's your take?"

"We know a few things for sure. Ronnie Tait was a fisherman. He died while working on a boat owned by Captain John Kemp, out in the Bering Strait. If they're doing something illegal, it's not going to be overfishing, is it?"

"No." Miller's hand rested on the door to the observation room.

"So it's either human trafficking or drugs, right?" As he said the words, a chill ran down Jock's spine. If he was correct, whoever wanted Phoebe dead would stop at nothing to protect their operation.

EIGHT

Jock's heart sped as he followed Miller into the observation room.

A woman in a suit almost as fancy as that of Beau Thomas's attorney stood next to Chief Anderson, staring through the window. She turned, a frown on her face. "I don't like this."

Jock bounced his fist on the wall. "I don't think he'll be able to use that defense. He's hiding something bigger. I suspect he's involved in trafficking of some kind."

The ADA raised her eyebrows. "What makes you think that?"

Jock relayed what he'd explained to Miller, then said, "I think it's more likely drugs. Ethan Davis was high on fentanyl when he attacked Mrs. Tait. He could've accessed it through anyone on Kemp's boat, if that's what they were doing."

"Okay, if that's the case, we can show he recklessly placed himself in the situation. He can't use the duress defense." The ADA's eyebrows flashed up. "This is just a theory, though. I need evidence. You'll have to find out more before we proceed."

Miller leaned forward. "What do you want us to tell his lawyer?"

"Tell him no deal, we'll see him in court tomorrow." The ADA grabbed her coat and slipped it on. Jock gave her a curt nod.

Chief Anderson opened the door for her. "We'll continue to investigate and keep you updated."

The ADA reached out and shook the chief's hand. "Thanks. FYI, if you're right about this, the DA won't give Thomas a deal. We'll prosecute him for everything we can. He might get a deal on federal charges from the US attorney, though, if that pans out." She swept out of the room, headed straight for the entrance. Jock pressed his lips together. Federal charges were out of his jurisdiction. He'd have to involve the US Drug Enforcement Administration.

The chief frowned. "Miller, go tell Thomas's lawyer that we'll see them tomorrow at the arraignment."

Miller walked toward the interview room, and Jock made his way toward his desk. Bruce remained in his bed, where Miller had left him. His ears perked when Jock approached.

Jock slipped him a treat then picked up his phone, noticing a missed call from his mom. She'd texted him twenty minutes earlier: Phoebe's been discharged, please come get us.

He quickly texted back to give him thirty minutes, then dialed his friend at the DEA. If drugs were involved, the DEA might already be investigating. Or they'd eventually want to take over the investigation. But Ronnie Tait's death remained with the Cordova PD. The DA could still decide to sign a plea deal with Beau Thomas if he gave information relating to the state crimes, but Jock agreed with the ADA. It was a waste of time. Maybe he'd get a slightly reduced sentence if it came to it, but any prosecution for Ronnie Tait's death seemed a long way off.

Special Agent Cal O'Brien worked out of the DEA's Anchorage district office. They had worked together previously on a few cases when O'Brien needed local knowledge. They'd hit it off straight away, and Jock counted him as a friend.

"Jock, how's things?" O'Brien's slight Irish brogue still came through, even though the man had come to the US with his parents as a child.

"All good. Just calling about a case." He outlined his theory, along with the interview with the boat's captain and the threat to Phoebe. "What do you want me to do?"

O'Brien thought for a moment. "We're aware of fentanyl shipments coming into Alaska, but we hadn't flagged anything for Cordova. Definitely something we need to take the lead on. If you find anything related to the drug trafficking operation while you're investigating Ronnie Tait's death, let me know. In the meantime, we'll track down the captain in Oregon and share anything relevant to your case as well."

"Thanks, O'Brien. Do you want a copy of the case file?"

"Yeah, if you could send that through, we'll review it. Might be something we can connect up with our case. Look, I'll come to Cordova as soon as I can, but since it's just a theory, you're welcome to keep investigating on the ground. Just like last time." Sometimes locals were more likely to talk to local officers than a DEA agent from the city. The last time, that was exactly what Jock and another officer had done, smoothing the way for Cal O'Brien and his team.

"I'll follow up with the other crew members about Ronnie Tait's death and let you know if I find anything relevant for you."

"Sure, like I said, just keep me in the loop. Thanks for calling me first. If you're correct, this will help with my promotion."

Jock grinned. "Anytime." He hung up and stretched his arms over his head. The bruising on his shoulder seemed to have gone down, with only a slight twinge remaining. He needed to track down the other crew members from the original investigation reports: Mason Lane, Gavin Cheung and Todd Carnegie. But that'd have to wait. *Time to pick up Phoebe.*

Half an hour later, Jock walked through the entrance to the medical center. Reception explained that Phoebe, Charlie and his mom were waiting in a side room. *Thank You, Lord.* He'd feared they might've been exposed in the waiting area.

He made his way down the corridor.

Phoebe's voice came through the open door. "What happened to Jock?"

Jock paused at Phoebe's question. What kind of a conversation were they having? *I should interrupt.* Eavesdropping never ended well.

"It was my fault, really, as much as Dieter's." His mom's voice was full of regret.

He'd never asked his mom detailed questions about Dieter before. If he walked in now, she probably wouldn't give an honest answer. He lingered outside, stepping back to let a nurse pushing an empty bed by. The rattle of the wheels drowned out the first few words of his mom's reply, and he leaned close to the door, brushing against the white hand-sanitizer station.

"...expected that Dieter would treat Jock and Wallace as his own. In a way he did—he certainly wasn't shy about disciplining them. But he never loved them like a father would. Though he made a good pretense, that's for sure."

Jock ran his hand through his hair, thankful the nurse had replaced the bandage with a less obtrusive adhesive dressing. His mom had truly believed a man could love a child who wasn't his own? How wrong she'd been. He raised his hand to knock, wincing at the memory of the so-called *discipline.* Then paused again as Phoebe spoke.

"Don't feel too bad, I didn't exactly have good judgment when it came to choosing a husband the first time around. I won't make that mistake again." Phoebe sat up straighter. "I'll never bring a man into our lives."

Jock's chest tightened, and a weight of disappointment pressed on his heart. No man in her son's life left no room for Jock. Served him right for eavesdropping, and it was probably for the best. He straightened his posture. He shouldn't be feeling this way. Phoebe was a victim of crime, and he'd settled the matter before. Hadn't held out any serious hopes for a future with her. But when Miller had said all those positive words… It'd gotten him thinking. He sure wouldn't be thinking anymore. *Lord, You've given me Your answer.*

Half tempted to turn around and walk outside to clear his head, he swallowed, then gently knocked on the wall beside the door. "Just me."

His mom approached the door, her face upturned in a smile. "Here he is."

"Are you ready to go?" Jock forced a smile, glancing toward Phoebe, who still cradled Charlie against her. He looked sleepy now.

"Would you mind carrying Charlie for me, please?" Phoebe's tone was apologetic.

A sinking feeling entered Jock's stomach. Not like he could say no. "Sure. If he doesn't mind."

"Thanks." Phoebe smiled, and his resolve weakened. How welcome that rare smile had become.

He reached for the little boy, who didn't resist, but snuggled into Jock's arms and made himself comfortable. The warm weight of him made Jock's heart clench. *Lord, please keep this little one safe.*

They walked to the entrance, where Jock had parked. "Wait here." He passed Charlie to his mom and stepped outside. He'd left his vehicle close to the entrance. Only a few steps. But someone with a rifle could line up the shot easily enough. Jock carefully surveyed the area. He took a quick walk around the parking lot, checking for possible hiding places. *It looks safe.* They'd have to hope for the best.

Jock turned on the engine then stepped back into the foyer. "Let's go. Quick as you can. We need to move fast."

He helped Phoebe into the back seat with Charlie, while his mom rode shotgun. Jock kept his eyes roving, checking for threats as he pulled out onto the road.

So far, so good. They neared the edge of town, headed toward his mom's house. He glanced in his rearview mirror, wary of the headlights that flared behind them. Hadn't he seen that vehicle in the parking lot earlier? Jock's muscles tensed and he gripped the steering wheel. Could someone be following them?

Phoebe's arm ached, and she considered tapping into the stash of painkillers the hospital had provided. Not yet. She didn't want to be groggy. Instead, she concentrated on her son, holding Charlie to her with her good arm. Jock had strapped him into the replacement vehicle he was driving, but without a car seat, the toddler wasn't properly secured. Marge remained silent, her head turned to look out the window.

The revelation of Jock's childhood had shocked Phoebe. While Jock had mentioned something about his stepfather, she hadn't realized the pain he'd suffered. It surprised her that Marge had opened up about it, but that seemed to be her way. Unlike Phoebe, who tended to keep everything to herself. *Maybe I need to open up a little more.* Even Keziah hadn't known how Ronnie treated her.

She glanced at Jock. His jaw was set firm, and his eyes darted to the rearview mirror. Phoebe turned, checking behind them. The headlights behind them seemed to be closing in.

Jock sped up, and Phoebe's scalp prickled. Did Jock think that they were under attack?

Phoebe kept her eyes on the vehicle. Its headlights sped up too, closing the distance between them. Adrenaline ran through her bloodstream, and she clutched Charlie to her, supporting his head. The vehicle rammed them, and Phoebe gasped.

"What on earth was that?" Marge exclaimed, turning to see.

Charlie whimpered, no longer on his way to sleep. He clutched Mr. Snuffles tight.

"It's okay, buddy, just stay with Mama." Phoebe soothed the child, careful not to let him break free of her grip. How she wished she had the use of both arms.

"Mom, stay still." Jock glanced at Phoebe. "It'll be okay. I'll keep you safe." He radioed for help, pressing the accelerator to the floor. "I am under attack. I need you to send units now." He gave the dispatcher the location.

Phoebe's mind raced. She'd seen enough videos on what happened to the heads of under-four-year-olds on impact to have invested in a reverse-facing car seat for her son. There wasn't even a proper car seat in this police vehicle. "Jock—"

The dispatcher interrupted. "Units on their way, O'Halloran. Hang in there."

The vehicle rammed them again, sending them skidding

to the side before Jock could correct course. Phoebe's arm throbbed, and she pulled Charlie tighter as he protested. The poor thing had been so tired he hadn't uttered a peep since they'd climbed into the vehicle. She'd expected him to go to sleep. Now he'd been shocked awake. *Lord, if You're listening, please help us.*

"I don't like this, Jock." Marge spoke through gritted teeth.

"We're almost there. I hear sirens." The relief in Jock's voice made Phoebe's shoulders relax a little.

Phoebe turned. The vehicle behind them must've heard the oncoming police cars as well because when they reached the next intersection, the headlights swung onto the wrong side of the road and accelerated away from town. Phoebe strained to make out the license plate, but all she could see in the snow was the color and shape of the vehicle—a white Toyota Tacoma. Yet another popular vehicle. Only this one had steel bullbars on the front. No wonder it had been able to ram them so easily. Could well have been the same vehicle that pushed her and Jock off the road.

Jock radioed in the details, and Officer Garrison came in over the radio. "O'Halloran, you okay? I see you coming toward me."

"I'm fine, headed back to base now."

Garrison came online again. "I'll go after that vehicle for you."

"Thanks." He turned to take a better look at Phoebe, slowing as he did so again. "You're doing great."

Phoebe's heart raced. How could Jock remain so calm? His resilience sent a flutter of admiration through her stomach. She tried to ignore the ache in her shoulder where the seat belt had jerked her safely into the seat upon impact. Thankfully, Charlie seemed to be fine. Holding his head into her had helped. Had the Lord heard her prayer? *Thank You, Lord.*

Marge huffed. "No thanks to whoever *that* was. Jock, I swear, if you don't catch him soon, I'll take Caroline with me and do some investigation of my own."

Jock's shoulders tensed. "No, you won't."

Phoebe bit back a smile. Would she be so brave in thirty years' time?

Moments later, they pulled into the police station, and Jock parked. "Wait here. I'd like to check the damage." He jumped from the vehicle and walked around back. Even through the pattering of snow on the windows, Phoebe heard the low whistle he let out as he examined the vehicle's rear. Must be bad.

He came around to her door and helped her out. Carrying Charlie, he shielded him from the snow as they walked slowly toward the entrance. Marge had already stormed toward the building, greeted by Chief Anderson.

The howling wind buffeted Phoebe's hair, and she leaned into Jock to steady herself. They walked through the entrance, and the warmth made her sigh with relief.

"Are you sure you're okay?" Concern creased Jock's brow. A bruise radiated out from underneath the adhesive patch for the wound on his head. *Must still hurt.*

"I'm fine, thanks." That wasn't entirely true. Her head buzzed from the adrenaline, and her body ached. Emotionally, she was less than fine.

Chief Anderson strode toward them. "Are you folks okay?" He looked Phoebe up and down, as if checking her for damage.

"We're fine, Chief." In the fluorescent light, Phoebe could read on Jock's face what he wasn't saying. If the cavalry hadn't arrived when they did, it might've been a different story.

She held back a shudder. "Did they catch the guy?"

The chief let out a long breath. "Not yet. But we're working on it, don't worry about that." He locked eyes with Jock. "Miller's found something."

Phoebe's hands trembled. Would it be another death?

Jock rubbed the back of his neck, trying to shake the feeling of unease that tightened his chest. Phoebe needed to rest. She was one day out of surgery, and from the look of her, she'd barely slept overnight. But from the determined look on her face, she wasn't going to stop until they'd found whoever had run them off the road—not once, but twice.

His mom settled herself in the break room, and Jock handed over a very sleepy little boy. The child needed a nap, especially after the emotional rollercoaster he'd been through these past few days. Thankfully, the sofa made a nice bed for him, and he quickly settled down, his arm draped lazily over Marge's lap.

Phoebe had followed him, and she leaned to stroke Charlie's head and give him a kiss. "Sleep well, Charlie. I love you."

Jock gently rested his hand on Phoebe's shoulder. "You wait here while I check in with the chief." He needed to learn what Miller had found.

"I'd rather join you. You haven't told me what happened during the interview with Beau Thomas." Phoebe looked up at him, her brow creased.

"Sure, if it's okay with the chief." Jock drew a quick breath as his mind jumped to his theory about the drug trafficking. How much should he reveal? It was only a theory. If her husband had been involved in criminal activity, he had to confirm it first. He'd just have to tell her the facts and leave it at that. He stepped out of the room, waiting for Phoebe to join him.

"Thanks." She followed him to his desk. "I'm so grateful your mom is here." Phoebe lowered her voice. "Charlie has really bonded with her."

Jock's shoulders drooped. If he knew his mom, it'd be difficult for her to say goodbye to the little boy. He held his hand out, directing her toward the desk area where Miller and the chief waited.

Miller glanced between Phoebe and the chief, and the chief nodded for him to go ahead.

How thankful Jock was that the chief hadn't excluded Phoebe. He knew that Jock had been keeping her briefed along the way, but that didn't mean she could come sit in the meetings by default.

"Firstly, we attempted to track the phone that sent those messages to Mrs. Tait, but as expected it was a burner." Miller held up a hand in resignation.

Phoebe's shoulders drooped a little, and Jock resisted the urge to reach out to her.

Miller continued. "I also dug a little deeper into the crew manifest. One of the crew was never interviewed, and we only have his initials, not a name."

"What are they?" Jock leaned forward, fidgeting with his sleeve. How had the investigating officer missed that?

"C. A." Miller handed him the paperwork. "I haven't tracked down the other crew members, but I can keep on that if you need help."

"Thanks, Miller. I'll do that now." Jock wanted to track down those crew members and re-interview them himself. One of them might let slip what they'd been involved in.

Also, checking their alibis might help narrow down who could be attacking them.

Phoebe expelled an indignant breath. "Why would the captain not include the name on the register?"

Chief Anderson held out his hands. "Taxes. Immigration status." Thankfully, Jock could trust him not to mention the drug trafficking hypothesis. *That* was the most likely reason to leave the name off the manifest. Although the chief's reasons could be equally true.

"I can log in to Ronnie's contacts and check if he had anyone with those initials, if that'd help?" Phoebe gave an inward look, blinking rapidly.

The chief nodded. "Good idea. Go with O'Halloran."

Jock returned to his desk with Phoebe at his side. She sat in the chair, leaning her arm on the desk. Jock joined her, rolling his chair so he could reach the keyboard. He pulled up the timeline and quickly added the recent incidents, while Phoebe used her phone to check Ronnie's contact list.

By the time he'd finished the update and clicked through to the witness statements of the crew, Phoebe had drawn a blank. She lowered her head in defeat.

Jock patted her on the arm. "It was a long shot. Let's concentrate on the crew members we *do* know." He scrolled through the details.

Phoebe peered over his shoulder, and her long ponytail brushed his arm. "Do you think one of them might have been driving the white Tacoma?" Her voice held a hint of unease.

"Hmm, maybe. Once we track them down, we can check vehicles registered to them and their associates." He glanced at her, shifting in his chair. The warmth of her so close was too intense. "It may take a while. You should feel free to go hang out with Charlie and my mom if you want a rest. If I find anything, I'll let you know."

She yawned. "Maybe you're right. I'll take the chance while I can."

Jock reached into his drawer and pulled out a candy bar. "Here, that might help too."

Phoebe smiled. "I love that you have snacks literally everywhere you go."

The words caused a shifting feeling near his heart. She accepted the treat and headed off to the break room. *Get a grip.*

Jock grabbed himself a cup of strong coffee and after a few calls and another hour of research, he found Todd and Gavin. He learned they'd been working together on a hook-and-line catcher/processor in the Bering Sea since mid-January, based out of Nome. Or at least that was what the records said. He needed to get confirmation from the captain. Thanks to another friend with the US Coast Guard, Jock got the satellite phone number of the vessel.

The captain answered right away.

"This is Officer Jock O'Halloran from Cordova Police Department. I understand you have Todd Carnegie and Gavin Cheung on board?"

"What's this about, Officer? Are they in some kind of trouble?" The captain's harsh voice didn't sound happy.

No point spooking the men. While they might be charged with something later, Jock's primary purpose was to find out if they'd been involved in the attacks on Phoebe. "This is just a routine call. Their names came up in an inquiry. Can you confirm that they were working on board this past week?"

"Yes. They've been here since January fifteenth. We all

have. What's this about? Are they in trouble or not?" The captain seemed irritated now.

"Like I said, sir, this is just a routine call. I appreciate your help." He ended the call. At least now he'd narrowed down the pool of suspects. Assuming the captain of Ronnie Tait's crew really was in Oregon, Mason Lane and the mysterious C. A. remained the only crew members unaccounted for. Could Lane be the one behind the attacks? He had to find the man.

He quickly sent a message to Special Agent O'Brien, updating him on the alibis, then drew a deep breath. Mason Lane was a hard man to find. Finally noticing the time, his heart skipped a beat. It was past time Phoebe and Charlie were home.

He raced to the break room, only to find Phoebe sitting on the sofa with her feet up, reading to Charlie. His heart slowed. Phoebe had a thoughtful, slightly sad expression on her face, and the rings under her eyes appeared darker than this morning. Released from its ponytail, her hair cascaded over her shoulders. He cleared his throat.

She looked up with a small smile. "Look, Charlie, it's Jock."

"Juh!" Charlie grinned, pleased with himself. "Juh!"

"It's a work in progress." Phoebe winked.

Jock's heart reacted despite himself, and he grinned back at the little boy. *Stop it. There's nothing there for you.*

"Are you ready to go home?" While he'd been looking into the crew members, the chief had suggested he head home early, given his duty was effectively around-the-clock looking after Phoebe. He tried to ignore the little flip his heart had given at the thought of spending more time with her.

She licked her lips. "Yes. Marge got a lift home with Chief Anderson, so I guess she's feeling braver than me."

Charlie bounced the bunny on his knee, chatting away to it.

"I take it you didn't find anything new?" She gave him an expectant look.

Jock leaned against the doorframe. "I alibied out two crew members for the recent attacks. They're currently at sea, so I'll have to think about how best to interview them. As for the other known, and the one unknown, I'll get onto that once you and Charlie are settled."

"Thank you. I know it's a lot more challenging to work while you're taking care of us." Her chin quivered slightly, and she clasped her hands together in her lap.

"Not at all." Working wasn't the problem. His mutinous heart going where it didn't belong presented the real challenge.

Fatigue tore at Phoebe's body, and she could barely keep her eyes open when Jock drove them back home. Charlie was subdued, munching on the post-dinner snacks Marge had left for him.

Officer Garrison drove behind them all the way, and for that Phoebe was grateful. How she'd dreaded the drive home. The memories of being shunted by the assailant's vehicle so close to town made her shudder. Not just with her and Jock this time, but with Marge and Charlie. They *had* to catch the culprit, or else no one would be safe.

When they stopped at a traffic light, Jock reached over to grab a polishing cloth out of the glove compartment and wiped it over the dash.

Even though she was cradling Charlie in the back seat, her heart skipped a beat when his aftershave wafted toward her. *What's wrong with me?* No way would she allow this man into her heart. Even if he seemed so different from Ronnie, she would be unwise to risk Charlie's future on someone she'd just met. Especially after the horror story Marge had told about her foray into a second marriage. Marge seemed much more emotionally grounded than Phoebe, with a loving first husband, yet even she had been mistaken. How much more could Phoebe fall short?

As unpleasant as it was, she forced her mind to return to the present danger. Could she think of anyone who had the initials C. A.? Could the initials be deceptive? Like Ronnie being known as Randy to his friends? *Richard* could be shortened to *Chip*, or *Nicholas* to *Cole*. Ronnie had had a few contacts with *A* surnames. Maybe she needed to think a little more creatively. That'd have to be after she'd had some food and sleep.

"You want to put Charlie down for the night while I make dinner for us?" Jock spoke softly, his kind voice interrupting her thoughts.

Phoebe's shoulders sagged with gratitude at the thought of him cooking for her. Aside from Marge's recent meals, no one had cooked for her in a very long time. "Good idea. Your mom has given Charlie plenty of food."

He gave her a small smile when they pulled up in front of his house. "It'll be okay. We're making good progress on this case." Maybe his confidence would rub off on her, but after all that had happened it was difficult to hold out hope.

She forced a smile in return and waited for him to carry Charlie through the snow to the house. Garrison waited until they entered the house before turning around and heading back toward town.

Phoebe followed Jock into the bedroom, where Jock eased Charlie out of his coat and lowered him onto the bed. "Do you need help getting him ready?" he whispered as he placed Mr. Snuffles in the cot.

Phoebe swallowed as she looked at the sleeping bag zipper and Charlie's heavy, sleeping body. She could probably manage, but it wouldn't be easy. Getting Charlie tucked in quickly was the best way to avoid waking him in the process. "If you don't mind…" Phoebe handed Jock the sleeping bag. "He can keep his clothes on." She gently tugged off his boots. Marge or Beth had dressed him in a soft tracksuit this morning. With Marge having changed his diaper before she left, he'd be fine without pajamas.

Jock maneuvered the sleeping bag around Charlie's body, careful to keep his head steady. The little boy murmured in his sleep, but didn't stir when Jock lowered him into the cot and tucked the bunny in the crook of Charlie's arm. Jock kept his hand on the boy's chest for a moment before slowly backing away.

"You've done this before," Phoebe whispered, impressed.

He gave her a small smile in reply. "Do you want to freshen up?" he whispered.

Phoebe nodded, glancing toward the en suite.

Jock left, closing the bedroom door behind him.

A crack left in the curtains revealed the glint of snow pattering against the window in the outdoor spotlight. Anyone could peer in on them. She shuddered, quickly pulling the curtains closed. Charlie muttered in his sleep, and Phoebe paused. Would he wake?

The child gave a little cry. "Okay, Charlie, I've got you." She sat next to the cot, reaching her arm through the slats and placing her hand on his chest, giving him a gentle rub. He snuffled, then settled. Better wait a while longer. Her broken arm throbbed, and she almost reached for the painkillers. No. She'd managed so far, and she needed to stay alert. What if they had to evacuate? Couldn't be groggy. This wouldn't be forever, though, would it? Her arm would heal. Jock would catch the attacker.

What will happen if he doesn't? Would they keep coming after her? When Jock had explained that Beau Thomas had shed no light on Ronnie's death, she almost gave up. But Miller had found that clue. *C. A.* What had she missed? She sighed. No point tying herself in knots over the unknowns. Jock had proven to be a thorough investigator. She needed to trust him to do his job.

Charlie's breathing had deepened, and his body relaxed. Phoebe slowly reclaimed her arm and eased herself to her feet. Time to freshen up.

Twenty minutes later, Phoebe emerged from the bedroom to the welcoming smells of lemon and garlic. She approached the kitchen just as Jock opened the oven, pulling out two salmon filets crusted with herbs.

"You're right on time. Let me grab the spuds." He set the fish on the stove and reached in to get some baked potatoes.

"That smells amazing. What can I do to help?" Phoebe smiled.

"Grab some cutlery, if you want. Top drawer next to the dishwasher." Jock's easy manner helped Phoebe to relax.

They settled around the table, and Jock prayed. "Lord, thank You for this food. Thank You for protecting Phoebe and Charlie. I pray that You will bless them and provide for them always. Amen."

"Amen." Phoebe raised her head, her eyes softening on the man as she tried to ignore the inner glow that warmed her heart. "Thank you for that. It means a lot."

Jock smiled, lifting his fork. "You're welcome." He took a bite of salmon.

Phoebe joined him, enjoying the delicious flavor of the

perfectly baked fish. "Wow, this is amazing! I assume your mom taught you to cook?"

"Yep. She wanted us to be self-sufficient. My sister can hunt and change a tire as well as I can cook and clean." He started on his potato, having slathered it in butter.

"My mom was big on outsourcing. I'm not very practical, I'm afraid." Phoebe cut into her baked potato. A challenge with one hand unusable in its cast. She allowed the small pat of butter to absorb into the fluffy center.

"Maybe not, but you're resourceful." Jock looked up from his meal. "Not many civilians who'd grab a gun and start shooting after they'd been injured in an accident."

Phoebe blushed. What could she say to that? She tried to scoop some of the potato onto her fork, but the potato skittered away from her.

Jock placed his own cutlery to the side. "I'm so sorry—I didn't think. Here, let me help." He scooted over to her and set about carefully cutting Phoebe's food into bite-size pieces.

Her heart rate picked up as his hand brushed hers, and she averted her gaze, not wanting to accidentally reveal her feelings. Instead, she forced a laugh. "Wow, now I know how Charlie feels."

Jock grinned, giving a slightly apologetic shrug. "You want me to spoon feed you too?" He winked, and Phoebe felt her blush deepen.

"I think I'll be okay." She retrieved her fork and plunged it into a bite-size piece of potato.

He shifted back to his seat. "Did your mom work outside of the home?"

"Oh yeah. She didn't want to rely on my dad for child support. I was a latchkey kid from an early age. Mom worked in IT. Still does. She's quite high up in her field.

Though she'd have liked to have moved to Silicon Valley, I think." Another thing her mom blamed on Phoebe. Not aloud, but with hints. She didn't want to talk about her mom anymore. "What about your mom? I can't imagine her staying at home for long."

"She was a teacher until she retired a few years ago. Beth took over her class, actually." Jock had almost polished his plate clean. He sipped his water.

"That sounds so nice. Must've been lovely growing up here." The words were out of her mouth before she could think. After what Marge had told her, it wasn't so lovely for Jock. At least for the first decade. She stopped herself from apologizing just in time, remembering that Jock didn't know she knew. But she couldn't stop her cheeks from burning.

"There was a lot to like." His diplomatic reply sent a wave of sympathy through her. His fork lingered midair. "I don't want you to feel awkward, Phoebe. Mom told you a little about Dieter, my stepfather, didn't she?"

Phoebe covered her mouth with her hand. "Yes. I imagine it's taught you what not to do if you were ever a stepfather."

"I've never thought of it that way." Jock pressed his lips together. "I guess you're right. But I don't intend to find out." He shoveled the last of his food into his mouth, staring at his empty plate.

A little stab of disappointment pricked her heart. Not that she'd had any expectations or plans to remarry. No. She couldn't trust her own judgment. Though, if she *did* ever get to a place, wasn't Jock the kind of man who'd… No, it wasn't going to happen. When she took another bite of the salmon, it didn't taste quite as good as it had a few moments ago.

Before she could think of anything else to say, her phone trilled. Another unknown number. Her heart slowed. "Hello." She answered on speakerphone, giving Jock a pointed look. "Who is this?"

Jock got up from his chair, moving quietly to her side. He grabbed his phone out, pressed Record and held it close to hers.

"I know about your husband's death." The voice on the other end of the phone had been augmented with some kind of computerized sound.

"What about it?" Phoebe's pulse raced.

"Beau Thomas is a liar. I know the real story."

Phoebe pressed her lips together, stifling a gasp. She'd been right! There *was* more to Ronnie's death than an accident.

Jock motioned for her to keep talking, mouthing *police station.*

"Really? How about you come into the police station and give a statement?" Phoebe's voice wavered as her agitation grew.

"No police, I will only talk to you," the computerized voice answered.

Phoebe looked at Jock, who shook his head. This was her chance to find out the truth about Ronnie's death. Didn't he want her to take it? "Where do you want to meet?"

"Where it all began. At the harbor." *Where it all began? What does that mean?* Phoebe's heart rate picked up. Could this be the answer she'd been looking for?

NINE

Adrenaline raced through Jock's body, putting him on high alert. Who spoke on the other end of the phone? Mason Lane? C. A.? Should he intervene in the conversation? Probably. If not now, when?

"This is Officer Jock O'Halloran. I will be accompanying Mrs. Tait to the harbor, or she won't be coming." He held his phone closer to Phoebe's, mindful that the conversation could form part of the evidence.

The computerized voice paused. "Okay, you can come. But no one else. No other police officers. Just you and Mrs. Tait." Jock's suspicions rose. The person had agreed too readily to Jock's involvement. Agreeing to Jock coming along with Phoebe must mean the person was desperate to meet. But why? Alarms went off in Jock's mind. What information did this person plan to give Phoebe that couldn't be communicated over the phone? Were they walking into a trap? His instinct was to refuse. He did not want Phoebe anywhere near someone who would track her down and threaten her. Probably someone deeply unstable and dangerous, based on the attacks she'd endured so far. But there was a chance this person could help. Could that be worth the risk? It might be the best chance of tracking down Mason Lane and C. A. Either of them could even be the person on the other end of the phone. *I'll be with her, at least.* No way he'd let anything happen to her. A protectiveness filled his heart, and he had to resist the instinct to wrap his arms around her.

"Okay." Phoebe spoke before he could. "What time, and where?"

"Meet at the end of Nicholoff Way."

The spot was located a five-minute walk from the Cordova PD, at the end of a dead-end street. The caller must be confident about getting away. A sudden coldness overtook him. Maybe the caller planned to come by boat. He'd alert the US Coast Guard and have them on standby. Jock planned to arrest this person, no matter what. For Phoebe and Charlie's sake, he could not fail.

The voice continued. "Be there in fifteen minutes. I'll call you then with further instructions." Fifteen minutes didn't give them any time at all. No time to get backup in place. That must be the intention. Jock's gut churned, not for his own safety but for Phoebe's. Could it be worth the risk? Intercepting the caller would ultimately protect Phoebe, but if he meant her harm, Jock could be serving her up on a platter.

Phoebe's face dropped. "What about Charlie?"

Jock picked up his phone. "I'll call Beth. She won't mind watching him until my mom can get here." He glanced at Phoebe. "You'll need your warmest clothes, but I want you to wear a vest. Go grab what you need while I make some calls." The body armor would protect her if the attacker opened fire.

Phoebe gave him a look with a mixture of concern and gratitude and headed for her room.

Thankfully, with Cruz home for the week, Beth was only too happy to come watch Charlie until Marge arrived. A few minutes later, she was hugging Phoebe goodbye. "I'll take care of your son. Don't worry about a thing."

"Stay safe." Beth gave Jock's arm a gentle squeeze and locked the door after them. He didn't have to worry about Charlie with Beth in charge. She knew better than most the importance of personal security, having once been a target of an organized-crime gang. He noticed with some relief that Cruz had armed her with one of his favorite pistols.

Jock adjusted his beanie, pulled out of the driveway and called Chief Anderson.

"I don't like it," the chief said. "But if the coast guard's on standby, I'd feel a lot better. I'll call them, you concentrate on getting there safe. If it even smells like something might not be right, leave immediately."

"Yes, Chief." The chief's support lifted a few ounces of weight off Jock's shoulders.

But he wanted to update O'Brien. If he spoke carefully, he wouldn't alert Phoebe to the DEA involvement. "I need to make one more call." He autodialed from his recently called numbers.

Phoebe gave a vague nod, her hands clasped in front of her.

"What do you have for me, Jock?" O'Brien answered after the first ring.

"We're meeting an informant at the harbor. Thought you might want to stand by in case I make an arrest."

O'Brien scoffed. "Now? Hasn't the snowstorm come in yet? It's already hit us."

Sleet slapped against the windshield, and Jock's vehicle slid on the icy road. "Not yet, but it's on its way." Anchorage lay about a hundred and fifty miles northwest of Cordova, so they had some time. Hopefully it would hold off until they'd had the meeting. Last thing he needed was to get caught in the middle of a snowstorm with Phoebe. Not that he hadn't been caught before, but it would complicate any arrest.

"Keep me updated. I'll try and head to you once the storm's passed."

"Thanks, O'Brien." He ended the call and glanced at Phoebe, whose furrowed brow suggested she had a lot on her mind. *At least it's distracted her from asking questions.* Why had he said that he wouldn't be a stepfather? Sure it may be the truth, but he didn't need to say it. Wasn't like she had any expectations. She'd made her own plans clear—to his mom, at least. Had he imagined the slight disappointment in her eyes? Must've. Now, Phoebe's words from the hospital rang in his ears. *I'll never bring a man into our lives.* He stole a glance at the beautiful woman within reach of him. There was just something about Phoebe Tait that drove him to distraction. Even if she felt nothing for him, he couldn't turn his feelings off. He'd just have to deal with it because he was taking her into possible danger, and he knew deep down that she wouldn't accept no for an answer. No way he'd let anything bad happen to her, or Charlie. *Lord, I'm relying on Your help.*

"How are you doing?" He tried to keep his voice as neutral as possible.

She continued to stare out the window. "Is there really a storm coming? I haven't been paying attention to the weather forecast."

"Yeah, it's going to be a bad one. But we should be back home before it hits." Hopefully. At least their destination wasn't far from the police station. They could hole up there if necessary. There were foldout cots, blankets and supplies. As well as plenty of other officers.

"Hmm. What do you think the caller meant by meeting

at the harbor *where it all began*?" Phoebe took a short, fast breath before letting it out with a sigh.

Jock shrugged. "Maybe it's where he met your husband for the first time? I wouldn't read too much into it. He's probably coming by boat and wants an easy escape route. The coast guard is on standby, just in case. We'll catch him, don't worry."

Phoebe shook her head and turned to him. "That makes sense, I guess. But..." She sighed.

"It's okay, just tell me what you're thinking." Jock softened his voice, hoping that she still trusted him enough to share her thoughts.

"Doesn't it strike you as strange that you *just* interviewed Beau Thomas, and already we have someone calling to tell us he's lying? How does this guy know what Beau Thomas said? Surely only you, Thomas's lawyer, the ADA, the chief and the other officers know that."

Jock blew out a breath, impressed that Phoebe had noticed all that. "You're right, but in a way, it's not that surprising. Beau Thomas doesn't strike me as a trustworthy person. Whoever called you probably thinks he lied to us, which is likely. Or that he said some things about the caller that would implicate them in some way. Probably just looking to set the record straight."

"Could've said that over the phone, right? Why the cloak-and-dagger stuff?" Phoebe stiffened.

"That's a good question. I'm glad we're meeting in person, though. Makes it easier to arrest them." He flicked on his indicator then turned toward the harbor. "When we get there, I want you to stay in the car. I won't put you in danger."

Phoebe frowned. "I don't like that idea."

"They could be drawing you into the crosshairs. They've

rushed the meeting in an isolated spot, just before a storm hits, to put us on the defensive. I'd be surprised if we *weren't* greeted with bullets." Not that he'd let anyone get the jump on them. He knew the harbor well, and even with the poor visibility, anything suspicious would stand out.

"They can't control the weather. It'll be harder to aim." Phoebe jutted her chin out.

Jock grinned, impressed with her courage. "Maybe that's true. But I'm not taking any chances."

She turned, nervously glancing out the back. With the pebbly film coating the rear windshield, she wouldn't see much.

"No one's been following us." They turned down Nicholoff Way, and Jock checked the time. One minute to spare. They'd make it. To whatever *it* might be.

Phoebe's heart hammered like it wanted to leap out of her chest. Not that it could with the body armor strapped firmly to her torso. While uncomfortable, she was grateful Jock had insisted she wear it. *I need to stay alive for Charlie.* Staying in the car wasn't an option. Jock must know that. The caller had barely agreed to Jock coming, let alone without Phoebe. They were almost certainly walking into a trap. But at this stage, Phoebe was willing to take the risk, and thankfully Jock was too. Living on edge, waiting for the next attack, wouldn't get them any closer to arresting the attacker. This meeting offered progress.

Sleet whirled around, buffeting the boats that remained moored at the small boat harbor. Even the seagulls had taken cover, no doubt anticipating the incoming storm. Though she grasped her phone, waiting for the call, she still startled when it rang.

"Answer on speaker again." Jock held his phone nearby, hitting record.

"Hello." Unable to stop the quaver in her voice, she steadied the phone by locking her elbows against her body.

"I see you." The computerized voice sounded clear, despite the howling wind. Maybe they had some kind of noise canceling microphone.

Phoebe searched the harbor but saw no one. "Where are you?"

"Walk down to the final berth on the dock closest to your vehicle."

Jock shook his head and gestured toward himself.

"Why can't you come to us? There's no one else here." Phoebe's heart picked up as the tension rose.

"No. Do as I say, or you will never hear from me again." The computerized voice spoke slowly and clearly, like it didn't matter either way to them. "But be warned. Whatever happens to Charlie next will be on you."

Bile rose in Phoebe's throat. "Charlie?"

Jock's eyes narrowed, and he leaned to Phoebe's ear. "He's bluffing," he whispered, giving her hand a squeeze.

How do you know? Phoebe wanted to scream. Beau Thomas had been prepared to kidnap Charlie to get her attention. How much more would a motivated killer be willing to harm her son if it achieved his goal—whatever that may be.

Before she could say anything, Jock spoke toward the phone. "If you make any more threats, we're leaving. The FBI can deal with you."

The voice on the line paused. "You have five minutes." The call ended.

Jock frowned, peering toward the end of the dock. Unless he had better eyesight than her, it'd be impossible to make out details in this weather. "I guess asking you to wait here is out of the question."

"Yes." This could be Phoebe's only chance to find out what happened to Ronnie and to stop whoever meant her and everyone close to her harm. She thought of Charlie's tiny body being discarded in a snow berm near the airport. Him clutching Marge as her house went up in flames. His whimper as their vehicle was shunted from behind. How could she risk that, or worse, happening to him again? Wasn't even a choice.

She pulled her scarf tighter, stowed her phone in her pocket and pulled on warm gloves. When she opened the door, a gust of wind blew sleet against her face. "We don't have much time, let's go."

Jock leaped from the vehicle and hustled around to her side, curling his arm protectively around her shoulders, partially shielding her body with his. "Stay close to me. If they open fire, hit the deck."

"Okay." Phoebe's adrenaline increased. Hopefully the snow would make it harder to take aim.

They walked along the dock, and it groaned and swayed as wind whipped waves on the surface of the harbor. At the end, a small fishing boat had been moored, uncovered—unlike those boats surrounding it, which had been battened down for the winter. Ice clung to the bimini and gunwale, and Phoebe shuddered at the thought of how slippery the deck must be.

She hesitated near the stern, and Jock placed his hand on his Glock. Just then, her phone rang.

The computerized voice spoke before she could say anything. "I'm on board a yellow fishing boat outside the harbor in Orca Inlet. There are binoculars on board the boat if you can't see me. Take the boat and sail toward me. The keys are in the ignition. I will wait for fifteen minutes, and then I'm leaving." The caller hung up.

Jock helped Phoebe onto the boat and sat her down in the cockpit. He grabbed the binoculars and pointed them toward Orca Inlet, adjusting the focus. "I see a yellow fishing boat out there, and it's lit up like a beacon. Definitely someone on board. I can't see them in detail, though."

Phoebe's heart rate picked up. "Do you think the caller's telling the truth?"

"No." Jock's jaw clenched, and he sucked his teeth. "Something feels off. I think we need to leave."

"What are you talking about?" Phoebe's eyes widened, and a feeling of trepidation came over her. "What about Charlie?"

"Charlie will be okay. I asked Cruz to escort my mom and Charlie to their place when Mom gets there. He worked in witness protection for ten years. He knows what he's doing." He frowned. "Ask yourself. Why the middle of Orca Inlet? It's bad enough we had to come to the harbor in this weather, but to meet someone we don't know on open water? I don't like it." He reached for his phone and dialed. "This is Officer O'Halloran. Chief Anderson called earlier." He listened. "Yes, that's correct. The fishing boat is yellow. Can't miss it." He listened then read out a number. "Thanks." He ended the call.

"Who did you call?" Phoebe's voice sounded strained, even to her.

"The US Coast Guard should be here in twenty minutes. They'll pick up whoever's on that boat."

Phoebe's heart raced. "What if they leave as soon as they see the coast guard's boat? We could go out a little way." A tightness had entered her chest. "You must understand,

I can't take the risk with Charlie. Maybe he's safe for tonight. But what about tomorrow night?"

Jock held her shoulders and turned her to him, looking her in the eye. "The coast guard won't let him get away. Please just trust me."

Phoebe pressed her hand to her heart. She *did* need to trust him. He'd given her so much leeway in this investigation. "Okay." She sighed. "Can we at least wait here and keep tabs on the boat until the coast guard arrives? If he sees us walk away, he'll know something's up."

"Let me check something first." Jock let his hands drop and walked toward the stern.

Phoebe braced herself against the seat, watching. Jock gently kicked the bulkhead, as if checking for something. His gaze appeared thoughtful. "Interesting."

She glanced toward the yellow boat that remained moored in Orca Inlet. "Twelve minutes." No sign of the coast guard. *Lord, please help me. I can't stand this.* A slight calm loosened her shoulders, and she focused on Jock.

He seemed deep in thought as he checked the deck. Running his hands over the joins, he tapped the fiberglass. Frowning, he pulled the cushions off the seats and rapped the seats with his knuckles.

The suspense was killing her. "What are you looking for?"

If Jock heard her, he ignored her, dislodging a crowbar. He held the tool up, checking each end, then stared intently at the deck.

She leaned in to watch him. He levered up some of the decking and let out an exclamation. He pulled out his phone and took a photo.

"What is it? Jock?" Why wasn't he saying anything?

"We need to get off the boat, now!" He reached for his radio, grabbed Phoebe by the arm and ushered her toward the dock.

Boom! A fiery explosion dislodged the boat's hull, knocking them to the ground.

TEN

Phoebe's ears rang, and she leaned heavily against Jock, who wrapped his arm under Phoebe's shoulders, dragging her away from the burning wreckage.

Black smoke billowed into the sky, overtaking the snow. The fire burned brightly on the dock, engulfing the boat in flames.

Jock gave her a gentle squeeze. "We're okay." His voice held a softness. Like he knew how fragile she felt.

She couldn't think of a response. What if Jock had listened to her? They'd be dead. Jock would've been collateral damage to her foolishness. Then that person in the yellow boat… What had Phoebe uncovered that someone wanted to blow her up? What had she missed in Ronnie's messages, or among his things? Did he have another phone or a computer she didn't know about?

Her head spun as Jock hurried her back toward the shore, half carrying her. Though his radio crackled, he was talking on thc phonc. Ilow hc managcd to hcft hcr with onc arm and have a sensible conversation remained beyond her.

"A yellow boat." He listened. "No, from what I saw, it was on a timer. I've sent a photo to the PD. They'll send it on." He listened some more. "Thanks, I'll coordinate with them." They were almost at the end of the dock now, their vehicle in view. "Are you doing okay?"

Phoebe's mind took a moment to process said the question. "I—I think so." She picked some stray pieces of fiberglass out of her hair. The acrid stench of burning plastic and fuel invaded her senses.

Jock helped her into their vehicle then climbed in, his head pressed to the phone. He blew out a breath. "Voicemail. O'Brien, it's Jock O'Halloran. You need to get here as soon as you can. They just tried to blow us up." He ended the call.

They just tried to blow us up. Phoebe's gut lurched as the reality of that phrase sank in properly. She and Jock should be dead. They'd escaped by seconds. *Thank You, Lord.*

Her mind turned to the perpetrator, and her chin trembled. "Who's doing this?"

Jock started the engine and turned to her. "We should find out soon. I've sent the coast guard to intercept whoever's on the yellow boat."

Lights and sirens came toward them, as fast as the weather would allow. Fire engines, paramedics, police—seemed despite the late hour, everyone had been called in. The heater began to warm her up, and she loosened her scarf.

"Wait here. I won't be long." Jock climbed from the vehicle, leaving Phoebe to calm her thoughts. *Charlie.* She picked up the phone and dialed Marge's number. Straight to voicemail. A chill ran through her. Why wasn't she answering? She redialed. Voicemail again. "Marge, it's Phoebe. I'm really worried about Charlie. Could you please call me the moment you get this message? Thank you."

Why wasn't she answering? It could be the weather. Jock had mentioned something before about the weather impacting the signal. He couldn't get through to that other guy. How she wished he'd come back so he could reassure her. More, she hoped he *would* reassure her. *What if something's happened?* The voice on the other end of the phone had madc that threat. Phoebe believed it. She tapped her fingers against the dashboard then rolled her shoulders. If he didn't come back within two minutes, she'd go join him.

Outside the car, fire fighters worked on the blaze. The fire and police chiefs spoke with Jock, who gestured toward the dock and showed his phone, shielding it from the snowflakes that were coming faster now. *Must be the photo.* How did Jock know so much about bombs? Another impressive quality. He turned, gesturing toward her, and said his goodbyes, walking toward the vehicle. Phoebe's heart flipped. *Lord, please let Charlie be safe. I'm counting on You.*

Jock brushed some snowflakes off his coat then jumped back into the vehicle. "Let's get back to Charlie."

"Jock…" Phoebe bit her lip.

"Yeah?" He reversed the vehicle, turning back the way they came. The windshield wipers worked hard clearing the snow from the windows. The weather promised blizzard conditions soon; they had to get home.

"I can't get hold of your mom."

He glanced toward her, his brow furrowed. "Let me try her." He dialed. Each ring lifted Phoebe's blood pressure a little more.

"Hi, this is Marge. Please leave a message." Marge's voicemail sounded just like before.

Phoebe felt like crying. "What's happening? Why isn't she answering?"

"Let me call Beth." Jock accelerated. He dialed, but the

phone went straight to voicemail. "I'll try Cruz." Same result. His shoulders relaxed. "It must be the signal."

"Phew." Phoebe rubbed her forehead, her heart steadying.

He glanced in the rearview mirror, and his phone pinged with a message. "Could you check that, please? It might be Mom."

Phoebe grabbed his phone from the dock. "Yes, it is. Want me to read it?" A message meant they were okay. *Thank You, Lord.* She read it aloud. "Charlie's missing." Her stomach lurched, and she forced herself to read on. "I'm at my house. Come quick." She drew a shaky breath. "At *her* house? Why? I thought she was with Jake and Beth." *Charlie!*

"Text her back, and we'll go by Cruz and Beth's place first." Jock gripped the wheel, flipping the windshield wipers up a notch as the sleet worsened.

Phoebe began to hyperventilate. "She needs help! What if he's lost outside? He doesn't have much time in this weather! We have to go to her now!"

Jock pressed his lips together. "Okay. Text her back that we're on our way. I'll see if I can get the chief on the radio. He can send someone by the Cruzes', though with all this it may take a while."

She typed the message with shaking hands, and Jock radioed in the update to the chief. The reply from Marge came back right away. "She says to hurry." A sickening fear lodged in Phoebe's gut. "Do you think someone's taken him? I don't understand how your mom would've let him wander off."

"I don't know. The chief has someone going around to Beth's to check. We'll get to Mom's first, so just hold on." He gave a slight grimace in her direction, which she guessed was probably to reassure her. It didn't.

While Phoebe had a lot of questions, Jock wouldn't be able to answer them. She also didn't want to distract Jock. With the snow picking up, the vehicle would take twice the time to get home now—even the lights of the town were obscured by the nearly whiteout conditions.

Instead, Jock spoke. "Do you have snowstorms in Tucson?"

"Not like this. I've never seen anything like it." Phoebe fixed her eyes on the flakes flying at the windshield, illuminated by the headlights. Must be freezing out there. *Charlie!*

"Did you grow up there?"

"Yes, born and raised." Phoebe swallowed. She appreciated him trying to distract her, but she couldn't think of anything but her son.

"Ronnie too?" His voice didn't hold an agenda, just curiosity.

"Yes," she snapped. *It's not Jock's fault.* She drew a deep breath. Maybe a distraction would help. "The company he worked for at the time had been contracted to refurbish the dance academy where I was studying. That's how we met." Her gut churned at the fact that Ronnie had brought them here. Now, Charlie… She tried to keep the bitterness out of her voice. "He was a real charmer."

Jock frowned. "I can imagine."

Phoebe's heart shrank. Their meeting had ultimately resulted in Jock's life being turned upside down too. "I'm sorry I brought all this to your doorstep. If I could go back, I wouldn't even come here. I'd just let Ronnie's memory alone." She scoffed. "I'm sure your mom feels the same right now." Tears welled in her eyes.

Jock's heart ached for Phoebe. The woman had so much undeserved guilt. *Lord, please help her to let go of her guilt and cling to Your mercy and grace.* "I don't feel that way, and neither does Mom. I can promise you that."

Phoebe swiped at the tears in embarrassment, and he suspected she didn't believe him. No wonder, given her treatment at the hands of those closest to her. Sounded like she'd spent her childhood being criticized, and her marriage hadn't been much fun. She wouldn't have high expectations of people in general. Maybe he could change that.

"I mean it. Mom's always taught me you can't love your neighbor like the Lord loves us if you're worried about a few bangs and scrapes along the way." Jock blew out a breath. Had he done all he could to help Phoebe? He still hadn't figured out what ongoing criminal activity had triggered Ronnie's death. Was now the time to say something? Relieve Phoebe of her guilt? No, they needed to find Charlie first. His mind returned to his mom. Didn't make sense that she'd take Charlie back to her house. But his mom did things that didn't make sense. What if she'd had some bright idea he didn't know about? What if Charlie was lost out in the cold? They couldn't risk it.

Phoebe just nodded. A sadness clouded her eyes. Jock's heart ached to see her like this—filled with sorrow and fear. He needed to try and distract her.

"Did you tell your mom about the stalker? The break-in?" Maybe the conversation would make the time go quicker.

She clutched the grab handle as the vehicle slid a little before the tires caught. Jock was used to driving in these conditions, but the weather sure wasn't doing them any favors today. The sooner they got to his mom's, the better.

"No. I don't tell her anything." She rubbed her hands on her legs. Just when Jock thought he'd have to reignite the conversation with more questions, she continued. "She didn't want me to marry Ronnie in the first place. Thought he wasn't good enough." She scoffed. "I know what you're probably thinking—'She was right, maybe you should ask her for advice.'"

"That's not what I was thinking." The silence dragged, and Jock's blood pressure ticked up. How he wished she would open up to him.

She gave a little sigh. "My mom wasn't nurturing like your mom. She's an immigrant and she had a lot of expectations from her own parents that she internalized. Plus, her personality. She's not an emotional person, quite cold, I guess you could say. Of course, unlike her, I wasn't really a very academically-minded child. Being an only child that kind of made it worse." She glanced at Jock, as if expecting judgment. "I mean, when I became a dancer, she practically disowned me. I have sympathy for my dad, in hindsight. She was just as hard on him as she was on me. Giving us the silent treatment. Belittling us when we didn't do things her way." She rubbed her hands on her arms. "But of course, I shouldn't judge her too harshly. I have her in me. I can be very cold and judgmental."

Jock turned, shaking his head. "I haven't seen that."

Phoebe hesitated. "Right now, I want to tell you to drive faster. Tell you that you're taking too long." She lowered her head into her hands. "We're here talking, when Charlie could be out there. Freezing..." She sobbed. "I just I couldn't let it go. I wanted to be better than her. She didn't try hard enough in her marriage to my dad. She could have done a lot of things differently. I promised myself I'd never be like that. I never wanted to let Ronnie down or make him feel like I didn't care for him above myself. So here I am. Trying to compete with my mom." She sobbed again, wiping her eyes with her sleeve. "And Charlie's..." Her voice trailed off into a sob.

How Jock wished he could hold her. Take away all the fear and the pain. The damage that so many had done to her. "No one could accuse you of not trying your best, Phoebe. I mean, here you are, winter in Alaska, risking your life for answers."

"Yes, but I've failed. Again. But worse, I've failed Charlie." She let out a small sob, swallowing it down. Jock's heart ached for her.

Phoebe's feelings were mighty familiar to him. Aside from the physical punishments Dieter had carried out when his mom wasn't around, the man's snarling, sarcastic voice remained seared in his memory. Even when Dieter had left, Jock had clung to victimhood during his angry teen years. He'd made a habit of blaming Dieter for whatever situation came up, until he'd learned the importance of forgiveness. That Dieter's sins had been against God, as much as against him. Could Phoebe hold on to that kind of blame toward her mom? If so, it was a larger burden than she knew.

He couldn't let her suffer when there was something he could do to help. His phone rang before he could blurt out something he might regret. "O'Halloran."

"This is Cody Hannigan from the US Coast Guard." Cody's voice sounded more enthusiastic than the other man he'd spoken with earlier. "Just calling with an update on your suspicious vessel. We boarded without incident. Found no human life, just a mannequin tied to the bridge." He gave a snort of amusement. "Can you believe it? A mannequin? If I didn't know better, I'd think it was a prank."

Jock stiffened. A bomb was hardly a prank. "Dressed as a fisherman? Plaid shirt and brown slicker?"

"That's the one. We'll keep an eye out for suspicious

activity. But, ah, yeah, no human activity. Plenty of sea otters, though."

Jock's heart sank. No wonder the caller's voice had been crystal clear. He'd been on land the whole time. "Thanks for your help. Sorry for wasting your time."

"Not at all. Happy to help. It's a fresh twenty-eight degrees out here. No tourists or fishermen, just wildlife. No better time to be on the water." Cody sounded like he meant it. "Besides, we're towing the boat back so CSI can investigate further. They'll update you."

Jock ended the call and turned back to Phoebe, whose anxious face confirmed that Cody's cheerful attitude did little to help.

"You understood all that?" he asked. The call had been on speaker.

Her mouth drew down. "Do you think Charlie's hurt?"

"No. He's a tough little kid. He couldn't have gotten far. We'll find him." He swallowed, skirting dangerously close to words he shouldn't speak. No, he needed to say them. "I promise."

Phoebe let out a breath and gazed out the window. Had she heard him? *Lord, I don't know what You want me to do here.*

They were past the outskirts of town now, and headlights appeared behind them. The vehicle went to pass them on the left, and Jock slowed a little to let them by. Only when he checked his side mirror, he noticed that the vehicle was the white Tacoma—its steel bull bar visible in front of its headlights!

Jock's gut lurched. There wasn't the option of outrunning the larger vehicle, and even if they did, where would they go? He could hit the brakes and shoot at the Tacoma, but with Phoebe next to him, it was too dangerous. His mom's street loomed up ahead. If they could reach home safely, they'd be able to take cover.

The Tacoma maneuvered to his right, then accelerated until it drew up next to Phoebe's window. Jock reached for his radio, intending to call for help. But rather than the truck pulling ahead, the driver's side window wound down, and the muzzle of a shotgun protruded. Jock slammed on the brakes as a blast rocked the cabin of his vehicle.

ELEVEN

The window next to her shattered, and Phoebe shrieked, adrenaline coursing through her.

Jock reached to shield her, pressing her back in her seat, away from the gaping window. He was forced to maneuver the vehicle with one hand. “Are you hit?”

“No.” Her face stung, and when she reached to touch it, her hand came away with blood. Must be from the glass. The earlier cuts had barely had a chance to heal.

The vehicle lurched toward them. Jock took back his arm and accelerated away from the white truck. It followed closely, its engine revving. Another blast hit their vehicle, this time the rear windshield. The icy outside air sucked any remaining warmth from their vehicle, chilling Phoebe's face. Snowflakes stung her cheeks and tangled in her hair. Thankfully, she'd kept her coat and gloves on for the ride home.

Jock yanked the wheel toward Marge's driveway. Caroline's white Chevrolet Silverado was parked out front. But the house remained unlit. “Maybe the power went out?” Jock's words echoed Phoebe's thought.

They pulled up behind Caroline's pickup. Caroline emerged with a shotgun held aloft. She pointed it at the vehicle behind them and fired. Glass shattered, and the engine of the white pickup revved again as it reversed away quickly.

"Of course Caroline is here." Jock breathed the words, anxiously watching the truck fishtail onto the road. He parked in the driveway behind Caroline's pickup and turned to Phoebe. "Mom must be inside. Go find her and I'll call this in. Maybe someone can intercept the vehicle. The chief may have some news on Cruz and Beth too."

"Okay." Phoebe had already unclipped her seat belt. She was out the door, racing toward the house without hesitation.

Caroline greeted her on the step. "Come on, let's get you inside. I just made some hot cocoa." The woman wrapped her arm around her as she made her way through the snow to the entrance.

"Hot cocoa? Where's Marge?" The hairs stood on the back of Phoebe's neck.

"She's out back searching for Charlie. Told me to stay here and watch for you. Power's out." The woman bustled her toward the front door. Phoebe didn't like the way Caroline kept her hand on her back. Hopefully, Jock wouldn't be long.

She glanced back toward the driveway. The snow had already obscured all signs of the white truck. Jock remained in the vehicle, on the radio. "I'll go help her. Please let Jock know where I am when he comes in."

Caroline closed the door. "You sure bring the drama with you, Mrs. Tait." Phoebe couldn't tell if her tone sounded light or sarcastic. The woman remained a bit of an enigma. Still, with so few people available to help, she had to be grateful toward the woman for once again coming to Marge's aid in a time of need.

"I'm so glad you're around. I don't know what we would

have done without you." Phoebe banged her feet on the mat, trying to dislodge as much snow as possible before it melted onto Marge's foyer.

"Don't worry about that. Just come sit down on the sofa. I'll go fetch some cocoa." Caroline gestured to the familiar lounge that Phoebe had sat in on her first visit to Marge's house. Now, a fire crackled in the hearth.

"No, really, I need to help Marge." Phoebe headed for the back door. She turned the handle. Locked. *That's strange.*

She unlocked the door, stepping out onto the porch. An icy blast hit her in the face, swirling around her and buffeting the open door. No sign of Marge. No sign anyone had been out here at all. Phoebe's mind raced. Where was Charlie's diaper bag? Marge had previously deposited it near the sofa, along with his blanket. If Marge wasn't here, then where was she? She went to go back inside, but a blast of wind slammed the door shut behind her, making her jump.

Reaching for the door handle, she paused. Hold on. Why was *Caroline* here? What did she even know about the woman? She hadn't said much about herself. The only information she'd learned was from Marge. Apparently, Caroline kept to herself and had few close friends and no family to speak of. Marge had also said that wasn't unusual here in Alaska. A lot of folks came to get away from people. Understandable. More than once in her life Phoebe had wished she could leave her surroundings and find a desert island just to get away from her life.

She considered what had happened since she'd reached Cordova. Caroline had been at the scene of the fire at Marge's house. Aside from whoever was in the gray truck, no one else was there. According to Jock, she'd shown up at Kyle Smith's murder.

Phoebe shook her head. *She's Marge's friend.*

Still…it'd explain why Caroline had been so quick to agree Phoebe should stop looking into Ronnie's death. It might explain those strange comments about Ronnie, making her feel guilty for bringing her problems to Marge's doorstep. Sure, she had a point, but she'd been the only one blaming Phoebe, outside of Phoebe herself. She considered what else she knew about the woman. She'd been in the navy. A sick feeling rose in Phoebe's stomach. She'd probably have the skills to rig the boat with a bomb.

The initials, C. A. Phoebe didn't know Caroline's last name, but the *C* fit. *Surely not.* No one had said anything about Caroline going out with the fishermen. Someone would've noticed, wouldn't they? Not if she was keeping it a secret and killing anyone who might compromise that. *Oh no!* Phoebe's heart hammered. Surely, she wasn't trapped in a blizzard with Ronnie's killer? No, she wasn't trapped. She had Jock. *I have to warn him!*

Phoebe rushed toward the back steps as fast as the wind would allow. Her feet slipped on the ice, and she slid into the railing with a jarring bump. If Marge wasn't here, how had she sent the text? And why? Had Caroline managed to spoof her number? She'd have both Marge's and Jock's details. If she'd been able to conceal her identity from the police technicians, that wouldn't be hard. Her heart leaped. Did this mean Charlie remained safe with Marge at Beth's house? She had to know.

Phoebe grabbed the railing as a gust buffeted her against the stairs, threatening to push her off her feet. Her broken arm jarred painfully against her, making her gasp. The slap of snow against her face drowned out the wind, which whipped her hair into a whirl. Reaching the yard, Phoebe crouched against the shrubbery, ignoring the pain of her frozen, cut-up cheeks. She had to get to Jock. He was armed. He could overpower Caroline and get some answers. Battling against the wind, she struggled through the snow drifts that had formed over Marge's garden. She made her way around to the side of the house. *Keep going.* The storm seemed to become more intense. Even the trees had been stripped of their fallen snow, with branches flapping like flags as the weather transitioned into a blizzard. Her face and arm ached, and her jacket seemed paper thin against her. She pressed on, one step at a time, drawing closer to the front yard. Would Jock still be there? The lights of the police vehicle strobed through the swirling white. Almost there. She squinted toward the vehicle. He remained in there, the light on, illuminating his face. He spoke into the radio.

"Jock!" She screamed as loud as she'd ever screamed, but the wind snatched the words before they could reach him.

Something made her turn. Caroline! Before she could react, the woman pressed a shotgun into her ribs. Her eyes were flinty, her mouth in a thin line. "Get inside. Now."

Jock's hands had seized. He reached into his pockets, pulled out his gloves and slipped them onto his hands. As they warmed, pain shot through his fingers. Too bad.

Jock spoke into his radio. "Chief, I need to go inside to help." While Phoebe, Caroline and Marge would already be out searching for Charlie, he couldn't remain in the vehicle.

Chief Anderson had grounded him where the signal was strongest. The wind was playing havoc with the comms. He'd been on the other end of the radio the entire time, sending out more units to assist after they'd finished things up at the harbor. Sounded like the best they could do was preserve the evidence and wait for the storm to pass, which the firefighters had helped accomplish quickly. Thankfully the bomb had been easy to disable.

"Stand by, O'Halloran," the chief responded. Jock ground his teeth.

His phone rang. "O'Halloran."

"It's O'Brien. I got your message. What's going on? Are you and Mrs. Tait all right?" Agent O'Brien's voice held a measure of concern. "You said a bomb went off?"

"Yes, it did, but we're fine." Jock stared at the house, anxiety rising. He needed to go in after Phoebe.

"I have something for you. Remember I sent my guys down to interview Captain John Kemp in Oregon?"

Jock leaned forward, straining to hear over the blizzard. "Yeah, I remember. Dungeness crab season."

"That's the one. They hauled him into our Oregon office. Gave him the whole nine yards." O'Brien paused, perhaps for effect. "They got him to confess to everything. Well, almost everything."

"What? What do you mean?" Jock's mind raced. Had he been correct about the drug trafficking?

"You were right, it's a drug operation. They've been running fentanyl with an expat from the navy. The expat works for some legal drug manufacturing establishment in China. Doubt the business even knows what they're doing on the side. Kemp handles things this end."

"How did that happen?" Jock could not believe a veteran would work to funnel poison into the country. "Why hasn't anyone stopped this?"

"We'll be doing something, don't worry. Anyway, Kemp wouldn't give us a name, above the initials C. A. He says this C. A. individual made him get rid of Ronnie. It wasn't an accident, O'Halloran. They murdered him. I don't know how yet, but we'll find out. We're not done with Kemp."

O'Brien's voice sounded grim. "Whoever's in charge is ruthless. A real piece of work. Only Kemp and one other guy, Mason Lane, know who this C. A. is. We'll track Lane down and interrogate the two of them until they spill."

Jock nodded as he took it all in. "Got it. Thanks, O'Brien. I'll let the chief know."

"Watch your six, O'Halloran. I have agents on the next plane to Cordova, but they'll be delayed by the weather. I'll be there as soon as I can. I'll keep you updated. But be careful, Jock. You're up against a dangerous, highly motivated killer." O'Brien ended the call.

The radio crackled. "O'Halloran, Miller has managed to get through to Cruz. He and Beth have Charlie and your mom with them. Cruz thinks there may be a cell phone jammer somewhere nearby."

A feeling of dread pooled in Jock's stomach. If they had Charlie and Marge, then… *Caroline Armstrong. C.A.* "I have to get inside. Caroline Armstrong is C. A. She's lured us here, and she has Phoebe. Send help!" He didn't wait for a reply, throwing open the door and jumping out. Blades of icy wind howled at him, pelting his face with snowflakes. He licked his lips, bracing himself against the vehicle. He'd left Phoebe with the person who'd murdered her husband! Would she still be alive? *Lord, please let her be alive.*

Bang! The sound of a shotgun blast cut through the blizzard. Jock turned to see Phoebe fly through the air and collapse to the ground. Caroline stood at the side of the house, her shotgun aimed at Jock. Bile collected in his throat. *Phoebe!* No longer caring about his own safety, he raced toward Phoebe. *Lord, please! I can't lose her!*

He skidded toward her, falling to his knees as he reached her. She lay limp, her arms and legs splayed. Her wet hair flapped in the wind, and her face was pressed into the snow.

A large hole in her jacket under her right shoulder blade evidenced the shotgun round. He gently rolled her onto her side so she wouldn't suffocate, careful not to move her spine too much. Pulling off his glove, he reached for her neck. Her pulse was strong. No blood. The force of the blast must've winded her to the point she'd passed out. Thankfully, the vest had saved her life, even if she'd have some cracked ribs and extensive bruising to show for it.

By the time he'd reached for his own weapon, Caroline had already come over, her shotgun aimed at his head. "Drop it!" The predatory coldness in her eyes was like nothing he'd seen from the woman before. "And the radio."

He threw his Glock away, and it sank into the snow, then he unclipped his radio and did the same. *Lord, I cannot do this alone. If Caroline plans to kill me, You will need to step in to delay her.*

Jock looked her in the eye as snow swirled between them. "Are you going to kill me right here in my mom's front yard? Really?" He raised his voice to be heard.

Caroline stared at him for a moment before throwing him some heavy-duty cable ties. "Cuff yourself." She growled the words.

Thank You, Lord. Jock cuffed himself.

"Into your truck. We're going for a ride." She gestured to Phoebe. "Leave her. The weather will finish her off."

"Please, at least let me bring her in the back." *Lord, please.* A plausible reason came into his mind. "Officers are on the way. If they find her here, they'll know your identity." Never mind they already did—Caroline didn't know that, and it may keep them alive long enough to escape.

Caroline frowned, pressing her lips together. "Okay. Get in the truck. Leave her to me."

Jock's limbs were shaky. He staggered through the snow

toward his truck. The door remained open, flung wide by the wind.

Caroline stayed behind him, the shotgun aimed at his center mass. “Get in.”

Something fell from Caroline’s pocket. A metal box with about twelve antennae. *A signal jammer.* One that big would block all GPS, cell phone, Wi-Fi and just about any other signal emissions within about one hundred feet. Cruz had said something about a signal jammer to the chief. That explained the lack of communication. *She’s been planning this for some time.* Putting one of those in his patrol vehicle would stop anyone tracking them via the GPS. *Unless I can kick it out of the car.*

As if reading his mind, Caroline glanced at Jock, her lips pressed together in another grimace. She bent down to retrieve the signal jammer, and Jock took his chance. He threw his body at the woman, aiming for her legs. She slammed to the ground with a furious grunt, and Jock rolled off her, scrabbling to his feet. He kicked the shotgun out of the way. Not like he could use it with his hands bound. Caroline crouched, getting to her feet. Jock lined her up, then hesitated. It felt wrong to kick a woman.

Caroline used his hesitation. Her leg shot out, buckling Jock’s legs out from under him. He fell to the ground, unable to break his fall thanks to his bound hands. All he could do was roll out of the way, toward the vehicle. Maybe he could get to cover. At least break the signal jammer. The sound of Caroline’s heavy breathing pressed him into action. This time he wouldn’t hesitate. *It’s her or me.* Her or Phoebe. No contest.

Jock pulled his legs to his chest, ready to launch himself at her again. But the click of a pistol made him stop.

Caroline held the gun two feet from his head. "I said get in the car!"

He eased himself to stand, then sat in the front. Out of the corner of his eye, the signal jammer remained lodged in the snow. *Maybe she'd forget about it.* Before he could swing his legs into the car, the distinctive buzz of a Taser being deployed sounded, and pain shot through his body. He buckled, convulsing, and Caroline's face came into view. She raised the butt of her gun and smashed it against his head.

TWELVE

The fuzziness in Phoebe's brain wouldn't leave. Could this be a dream? No, not with the throbbing pain throughout her body. She vaguely remembered Jock getting out of his car. Her plan to run for cover. Then the shattering force of something from behind. Propelling her face-first into the snow. She couldn't breathe. Must've blacked out.

When she tried to reach to rub her eyes, her hand wouldn't cooperate, and a shooting pain stabbed through her left arm. She drew in a deep breath, and her whole torso protested. *What's happened to me?* The throb of her arm reminded her: broken. The rest of her body… She remained still for a moment. Had Caroline *shot* her? Is that what propelled her forward?

"How am I still alive?" she whispered. Then she remembered the body armor Jock had insisted she wear. *Jock.* Where was he? Where was *she*? The sounds of an engine rumbled into her consciousness, along with the howl of the swirling, powdery wind. If she was in a vehicle, how was snow slapping against her chin? Didn't seem to be moving. She listened. The vehicle sound wasn't nearby. Not accelerating. Not even moving. Just a low background rumble. Why couldn't she see anything? She blinked, and her lashes resisted. Something covered her eyes, but not her whole face. Scratchy, like wool. Maybe her beanie? That was what it was.

Must've fallen over her eyes. She gingerly raised her arms, wincing as pain stabbed her. Didn't matter. She forced her hands toward her face, biting her lip as the pain in her arm intensified. Pushing the beanie up her forehead, the whirling reality hit and she gasped. They remained at Marge's house. Jock's vehicle hadn't moved. The smashed-out windows let in the stinging flakes that pelted her cheeks, clinging to her hair.

Beside her, Jock was zip-tied to the steering wheel, his hands in the ten-and-two position. His head sagged to the side, and she spotted a large welt on his temple. *Not another concussion.* Marge would be beside herself when she saw that. That thought sent a shiver through Phoebe's chest, and she whimpered at the movement as a lump dug into her back. Could it be from the body armor? Must be. She'd seen something about back force deformation on television. Could she wriggle out of it? Give herself some relief from the pain? Movement caught her attention. An icy film crusted the windshield, slightly obscuring Phoebe's view. She peered through the haze of swirling white, making out a hunched figure. *Caroline.*

The woman bent in front of the vehicle, and some muffled metal clangs rang out. She stood, stretching her arms over her head, not bothering to glance at Phoebe or Jock. Then she strode toward the other vehicle and climbed in, slamming the door behind her with such force that snow dislodged from the roof. The engine roared, and Jock's vehicle lurched forward, pulled by Caroline's truck.

Phoebe's panic escalated, and another uncontrollable shudder ran down her spine, activating more pain. From cold or fear? Maybe both. Where was Caroline taking them?

"Jock!" Phoebe found her voice, lifting it over the howl of the wind.

He didn't even stir.

They turned onto the road, toward Orca Inlet. *Where's she taking us?* Why hadn't the woman just finished the job? She'd had no hesitation in shooting Phoebe once. Why had she decided to spare her life? *She hasn't.* The woman wasn't taking them on a drive for fun. She'd have a plan for their deaths. In the blizzard, she could just pull over in a remote location, and they'd soon succumb to the elements. But that wouldn't give her certainty. There was a possibility that they'd survive. *Maybe that's when she'll shoot us.* Unless she wanted to make it look like an accident. Could Caroline truly believe that she would get away with what she'd done? Maybe. What then? What would cause their deaths to look like an accident? They were headed for Orca Inlet. Phoebe's thoughts froze. Did Caroline intend to roll them off the pier? A sick feeling rose in Phoebe's stomach. *That's probably exactly what she's planning.* Tears pricked Phoebe's eyes. It made sense in a sick kind of way. Eventually the police would go looking for them. If the first responders were busy rescuing—her heart paused—*recovering* Phoebe and Jock, Caroline could use the distraction to escape. No doubt she had a boat somewhere that she'd launch, disappear. *It's a good plan.* But it wasn't over yet. Phoebe's mind returned to the church service. The pastor had looked her right in the eye, hadn't he? Had the Lord been trying to communicate with her?

"Lord," she gasped. "Did You mean what You said? Do You want me back, even after I abandoned You for all those years?"

The swirling wind was her only answer. What did she expect? Some kind of sign? Her heart contracted. Would the Lord accept her back as His child? Hadn't the pastor said that recriminations were the last thing on his mind when his lost son, Josiah, had returned?

Have I returned? The words of the parable returned to her, along with the truly repentant heart of the prodigal son.

"Lord, I don't deserve Your grace, but I surrender myself to Your Will. Whatever You wish to do with me, I'm Yours." The words came out of her in a rush, leaving her gasping for breath. Then time stilled.

A calm descended over her. *I'm going to get out of here.* For Charlie.

Phoebe glanced around the cab of the vehicle, trying to ignore the pain in her arm with every turn. She had to do something. Maybe if she could loosen the cable ties that bit into her right wrist and cut into the cast, she could slip her right hand out. With every movement her broken arm complained with a searing pain. She eased off her gloves. They might be keeping her hands a little warmer than no gloves, but they were soaked through and in the way. The pain finally overcame her. *I can't do this.* She blinked back the tears that promised to spill over. *Think.* Maybe she wasn't going to get loose, but at least she could try and work out Caroline's motivation. She was the *C. A.* they'd needed to find. What had she been doing on the boat with Ronnie? Had she drowned him? Caroline had sure succeeded in making it look like an accident.

Phoebe wracked her brain, trying to work out what Ronnie and Caroline had in common. Hadn't Caroline been in the navy? Ronnie hadn't had anything to do with the military. What about friends? Did Ronnie have any friends in the military? Not that she could remember—though that wasn't surprising given how little Ronnie had included her in his life. All that came to mind was Ronnie's uncle. Hadn't he served in the navy? Could *he* be the connection? Seemed unlikely. Caroline had to be twenty years younger than the uncle. Besides, the man had died a few years ago. He'd left Ronnie a few thousand dollars and that archaic painting of the Philadelphia Navy Yard in the mid-nineteenth century. Ronnie had hung the gilt-framed relic in the garage, and as far as Phoebe remembered it was gathering dust. That had nothing to do with anything and knowing Caroline's motivation wouldn't help them now. She had to focus. If she didn't work out how to escape soon, she and Jock would be dead.

Jock's body was heavy, and his head felt like liquid metal was sloshing around inside of it. Flakes of snow and waves of freezing powder pummeled his bare hands and neck and shocked him back to full consciousness.

"Jock! Wake up!" A woman's voice sounded above the whistling wind, along with the hypnotic thrum of an engine. He opened his eyes, disoriented. How'd he end up in his vehicle? *Oh no.* It all came flooding back to him.

Phoebe. He tilted his head toward the sound of her. She rode shotgun, her hands bound at the front with zip ties. Tension wrinkled her brow, and she stared at him, searching his face.

"You're awake!" A sheen of white crystals covered her from the snow that intruded through the nonexistent window to her right and the shattered rear windshield. It must be well below freezing in the vehicle. Were her lips blue? Hard to tell in the dim light that reflected from the vehicle that towed them.

He instinctively reached for her, but his hands wouldn't cooperate. Trying to sit up, he realized he'd been restrained.

Zip-tied to the steering wheel. The engine sound wasn't coming from his vehicle, but outside.

"Are you okay?" Phoebe's voice sounded weak, and Jock's gut contracted. Her teeth chattered, and she shivered. *At least she's shivering.* She might not be for much longer, if he didn't get her warmed up.

Jock needed to remove these restraints. He yanked at them to no avail. Caroline had used his police-issue zip ties. Short of a knife, he wasn't going anywhere. Phoebe could be bleeding internally from the impact of the shotgun. He needed to assess her. "How's your breathing?"

"Fine." She breathed in and out, demonstrating. The shivering intensified, and Jock's adrenaline spiked.

He tried to lean toward her to check her pupils, but he couldn't move. "Are you feeling dizzy? Nauseated?" He couldn't reach her to check her blood pressure.

"A little. Why?" The gale force wind buffeted their vehicle from side to side, and she winced.

He ignored her question. No use telling her she might be in trouble. "How's your pain level on a scale of one to ten?" She must be in terrible pain, unless the adrenaline was masking it.

"I don't know. Not ten. It hurts to breathe and to talk." Tears spilled down her cheeks. "Sorry, I don't mean to cry, but I'm worried we won't live long enough for it to matter."

Frustration at not being able to touch her bubbled through him. How he longed to take her in his arms and reassure her. Protect her from the weather and the fear. Instead, he had to gather the facts of the situation. "Do you know where we're going? Has Caroline said anything?"

"I thought maybe Orca Inlet, but she hasn't said anything. Last I remember she shot me, then I woke up here." A bump in the road made Phoebe wince.

Jock's throat constricted. They had zero information.

"Do you know why she's doing this?" Her voice rose as her distress grew, intensifying the ache in his head.

"No." He closed his eyes. No, he *did* know. But now wasn't the time to talk about it. They needed to get out of here. Given the direction they were headed, Jock suspected Caroline planned to ditch their car near the ocean. Probably into the ocean. The fact she hadn't already shot them both in the head puzzled him. Caroline hadn't had a problem shooting Phoebe. She couldn't have known that her target wore body armor. Phoebe was right to question why she hadn't just strapped them into the car then shot them. *Must be a reason.* Maybe she planned to hold them hostage to ensure her safe departure.

He struggled to get his hands free, the futility of the exercise concentrating his mind. If only he could check for the knife he usually kept under his seat. Could Phoebe reach it?

"Can you reach under my seat?"

Phoebe's mouth turned down. "Maybe. Why?"

"Can you please try? I keep a knife under my seat. If Caroline hasn't taken it, we can cut ourselves free."

"I'll try." She steeled her jaw.

"Okay, do your best." *Lord, please help her.*

With great difficulty, Phoebe unclipped her seat belt and turned in her seat. She gasped, and Jock's heart clenched. Must be painful. She bit her lip, reached down and somehow managed to reach the catch that slid his seat backward. A whimper escaped her lips, but she swallowed it down. Jock pressed his legs against the door to make room for her to reach under the seat. With hands bound, the action would be awkward for anyone. But with the added impediment of her broken arm, let alone her hands shaking from the cold,

Jock didn't hold out much hope for her success. *Lord, without Your help, we're not going to make it.*

Yet, somehow, perhaps muscle memory from her dancing, she managed to bunch her shoulders and overextend her arms until her hands disappeared under the seat. "I can feel something."

"Careful, it's a sharp knife."

She gasped. "Ouch!"

"Are you okay?" Jock's breath caught.

"Yes, I'm okay." A smile appeared in her voice. "Just a cut, but I'm free." She slowly sat up, one of her hands free, the cast arm still encircled in a zip tie, the knife held fast. "Let's get you free." Her quivering hands slipped on the knife as she clasped the steering wheel, and Jock realized how white her hands had become. She must be freezing. The fact she could even hold the knife was amazing.

She cut his right hand free, and as she winced in pain, he took the knife from her and released his left hand. Finally able to hold her, he drew her close, checking her pulse. A little on the low side, but nothing dangerous. Yet. He grabbed the blankets from the back seat and wrapped the first tightly around her. He draped the second over her lap, wrapping it around her legs.

"Thanks," she whispered, closing her eyes.

Jock focused on next steps. The vehicle wasn't moving at a fast pace. Maybe twenty miles per hour. If it were just him, he'd jump free from the vehicle and hope Caroline didn't notice. But she'd notice two of them, and then the shotgun would come out, and there was nowhere to escape to. They'd have to wait until Caroline stopped the vehicle.

As if he'd willed it, the vehicle lurched off the road toward the ocean, where ice-covered rocks loomed ahead. But rather than stopping, Caroline accelerated, then jerked her truck to the right, uncoupling Jock's vehicle with some kind of automatic release mechanism.

The tires slipped on the ice, and when Jock applied the brakes, they didn't respond. He yanked on the manual brake, but it flopped in his hand. Caroline must've disabled the brakes when he was unconscious. Holding his breath, Jock tried the steering wheel, but the tires were immovable, their course set on the ocean. He grabbed Phoebe and held her to him as the front of the vehicle tipped into the water!

Water filled the footwell, chilling his feet.

Next to him, Phoebe pulled her feet onto the seat. "Jock! We have to get out!"

Jock attempted to flip on the lights and sirens in the hopes of attracting attention, but they did not respond. He reached for the light in the cab, but it, too, failed. Caroline must have disabled the electrics for the whole vehicle. Fortunately, she couldn't disable the GPS tracker, which was battery operated. When the jammer ran out of juice, they'd be found. Eventually.

The vehicle slipped, the front submerged. *We don't have time to wait.* Jock's stomach hardened. He had to somehow get out of the vehicle before it filled completely. The icy water alone could kill them. Drawing a deep breath, he reached for the door and pushed. Water held it tight. The vehicle tilted, and water gushed in through the smashed-out window.

"Let's get out! Now!" He poked his head out of the window, but before he could get any farther, a bullet ricocheted off the window frame.

"Don't try anything, or next time it'll be a head shot!" Caroline had taken out a bullhorn, and her voice boomed and crackled through the swirling blizzard. Didn't look like the woman was going anywhere. How would they escape now?

THIRTEEN

Phoebe startled at the sound of Caroline's firearm blast, and Jock fell back into the cab with a splash. "Jock!" She gasped. "Are you hit?"

"I'm fine." His eyes darted around. Not quite panicked, but nearly.

The river of freezing water quickly submerged her waist. A briny smell enveloped the vehicle, and icy tentacles seeped through her clothes. The pain in her arm magnified as the water percolated through her cast. Before she could think, it was up to her armpits, floating her, pressing her toward the roof. Her drenched hair tangled behind her, snagging on the head of the seat.

Lord, am I about to meet You? The thought didn't fill her with the dread that death had held before. But Charlie…

Then Jock's hands found her, and he gripped her hand as the water came to her neck, then chin. "Hold your breath. I'm getting us out." He said the last words, and the icy flood covered Phoebe's face.

The temperature made her involuntarily let out more breath than she meant to as a fresh flush of adrenaline shot through her system. *Trust him.* The words entered her head, unbidden.

Jock's hand tightened around hers, and he pulled her,

leading her through the window. Her lungs burned. She couldn't do this anymore. Had to take a breath. But there was none to take. She opened her mouth, and it filled with frigid, salty water. *I'm going to drown.*

But Jock grabbed her hair, tilting her head so her face was above the water. She coughed, choked, spluttered as waves lapped over her chin.

Bang! A shotgun blast sailed so close that the slipstream grazed her cheek. Jock dragged her back under, pulling her after him. *Lord, I hope he has a plan.*

Just as she was about to lose her breath again, he pressed her to the surface. Disoriented by the darkness, she gasped for air. Would he pull her back down? This time, he pulled her to him, supporting her head above the water.

"It's okay. She can't get a shot." Jock panted from the exertion.

Phoebe glanced around. The rear of Jock's vehicle protruded from the ocean like an iceberg.

"The inlet isn't deep here. It won't go down any farther." He treaded water, and Phoebe realized he had been carrying both of them. Even weighed down by his heavy coat and boots.

Phoebe's teeth chattered uncontrollably, and Jock held her to him. Her heart raced as fast as her mind. *What are we going to do now?* Thoughts of slipping into the sea and drowning made her stomach contract. The salty water that dragged her down, chilling her body, must be doing the same to Jock. He couldn't keep this up for long. Would they drown first? Or maybe pass out from hypothermia then drown. Her eyes burned, and she wrapped her hand around Jock's back.

"We'll be okay." Jock's lips seemed tinged blue in Caroline's headlights.

Tears trickled down Phoebe's cheeks, like painful rivers of lava. "It's impossible."

With God all things are possible. The words appeared as if whispered in her ear. Like the words to trust Jock Where did they come from? Jock hadn't said anything. Had he? Her eyes widened. Maybe the *him* she needed to trust was actually *Him.*

Ask. The whispered words came again.

"Lord," she gasped. What could she ask? Her mind returned to the sermon. On God's mercy. What else could she ask? "Please have mercy on us." The prayer came out in a sob, and Jock held her to him, his cheek resting against hers.

When she didn't speak, he continued. "Lord, I pray that You will offer Your protection. Please keep us safe from harm. Send us help in this hour of need. Amen." His voice wavered, and he began to shiver.

"Amen." Phoebe forced out the word. She couldn't hold back the tears, and they flowed freely, painfully hot against her frozen cheeks.

Jock held her close, his lips warming her cheek as he kissed her. "I'm right here, Phoebe. I'm not leaving. We're in this together."

The comforting warmth of his breath filled her with a peacefulness that slowed her pulse. *We're in this together.* The only other person who'd said that was Keziah when they'd opened the studio. But that had been a happy occasion. A celebration that they were finally realizing their dreams. Never before had someone taken her in their arms during the dark times. Not like this. Never before had someone soothed her in a way that filled her with a sense of calm and safety like Jock was now. *Will this be the only time?* The poignant question brought fresh tears to her eyes. Only now, when she was about to die, could she understand the feeling of being loved and cared for by a man. But it came too late. She'd never get to know if she could have this with Jock. *Lord, thank You for allowing me to feel this, just once.*

A blinding light filled the area, and Phoebe squinted toward it. Was it real, or was this her body shutting down?

"US Coast Guard, drop your weapon!" The loudspeaker from the USCG patrol vessel blared over the blizzard. The boat scooted past Jock's vehicle and pulled in close to the shore. Two of the crew, guns held aloft, disembarked and headed toward Caroline's truck.

Jock shifted, turning toward the shore. "Do you think you can swim? She's going to try and escape. Here's our chance."

"I'll try." Her broken arm had lost all feeling, so she turned onto her back, holding it against herself. Jock did the same—his hand under her shoulder, gripping her coat as together they kicked slowly toward the shore. Phoebe felt like she was swimming in a slurry of icy molasses, her limbs weighed down as she flailed her legs as best she could. Whether she was making any progress on her own or relying entirely on Jock, she couldn't determine.

The light filling the area glowed and changed as blue-and-red lights approached. Phoebe wanted to see what was happening, but she needed to try and reach safety. All she could do—all she *wanted* to do—was to follow Jock. He'd lead her back to Charlie.

Jock exclaimed and grabbed her shoulders, pulling her up. "Found the bottom." He grabbed her hand, but her legs collapsed, and she fell against him with a cry.

"I got you." He tucked his arm around her waist and pulled her along with him through the chest-deep water. "Thank You, Lord." He swallowed. "Only He knows how they found us, but *I* know you and Charlie are going to be okay, Phoebe."

Phoebe's heart quickened, even as her body grew sluggish. He hadn't forgotten about Charlie in all this. The water receded the closer they got to shore, and out of the water, it became harder for Jock to hold her upright. As they got near the shallows, Jock staggered to the side. Members of the fire department were there, rushing to bring them in. One carried Phoebe to shore, and the other helped Jock, whose legs seemed to be failing him. Phoebe was suddenly so tired. All she wanted to do was close her eyes.

The fireman gently laid her down on the waiting gurney, and the paramedic wrapped a heated blanket over her.

She grabbed the paramedic's sleeve. "My son, Charlie. I need to know he's okay. Jock has the number."

"They're already calling. Should know soon." Jock's voice sounded next to her. "Check Phoebe for internal bleeding. She sustained a shotgun blast to the back rib cage. I haven't removed the vest."

"You need to lie down, O'Halloran. We've got her." The paramedic smiled at Phoebe. "How are you feeling? Any pain?"

"No." Phoebe could barely feel anything. Her body was numb, and her eyelids were heavy. *I'll just rest them.*

"Stay with me, Phoebe." The paramedic gave the middle of her shoulder a gentle squeeze.

Phoebe opened her eyes. "Charlie." Surely, Jock was right. He *must* be okay.

The paramedic was leaning over her now, her smile a little less bright. "Try and stay awake for me, okay?" She turned to her colleague. "Let's load her up."

"What about Jock?" Phoebe managed.

"He'll be right there with you." The paramedics loaded her into the back of the ambulance.

Phoebe glanced toward Caroline, who had been handcuffed and was surrounded by the police chief, another officer and the two US coast guards who had come to shore.

They had survived. Not by anything they had done. *Thank You, Lord. Please keep Charlie safe.*

Jock's legs grew weak, and he became lightheaded as the paramedics loaded him into the second ambulance. How thankful he was that they'd survived. For a while there, he wasn't sure they would. Witnessing Phoebe's strength throughout the ordeal had mined feelings that he hadn't experienced before. Her trust in him had spurred him on, even when he was sure he couldn't go on. The poignancy of the love he'd developed for this woman should leave a bitter taste in his mouth, but it didn't. Instead, he yearned to be close to her.

The ambulance slowly picked through the unplowed road to the medical center, and thirty minutes later, they arrived safely. Watching her being wheeled away left a tightness in Jock's chest that wouldn't loosen. He'd bonded with her in the past few hours in a way he couldn't imagine doing with anyone else. Didn't *want* to do with anyone else. *Lord, what do You want from me?* He rubbed his chest, wishing that would stop the pain. If only someone could tell him how to turn off his heart. How was he going to say goodbye to her?

An hour later, Jock's body protested as the doctors ran tests and gently warmed him. "If you'd been in the water another few minutes, I don't think we'd be having this conversation." The doctor's sober assessment filled Jock with a renewed thankfulness. *Lord, how grateful I am that You are in control. Thank You for answering my prayers.* He brought to mind Phoebe's face. *Lord, if it's Your will, would You find a way for me and Phoebe? Please? I don't think I can say goodbye to her.* How would the Lord fix his brokenness? How could the Lord help him to avoid the mistakes of his stepfather? If he couldn't trust himself, how could Phoebe trust him with her son?

Soon, the doctor left, and the nurse came by to check his IV fluids. He caught her attention. "Could you give me an update on Phoebe Tait, please?"

"I'll go check for you."

Beeps and alarms sounded every so often, and nurses' footsteps hurried to and from rooms along the hall. The night-shift nurses spoke in low tones as time shifted steadily toward daybreak. The pungent smell of bleach and disinfectant lingered, and the warmth of the space offered him some respite from the cold. How he hoped that Phoebe would be comfortable. Staying still wasn't Jock's forte, especially not with the ache in his heart he couldn't ease.

He pressed his buzzer, and the nurse returned. "Mrs. Tait is resting. The doctor is monitoring her closely."

Lord, please heal her. "Thanks. Could I make a call, please?" He'd lost his phone somewhere. Probably at the bottom of Orca Inlet by now.

The nurse helped him get a line out, and he dialed his mom.

"Jock! Thank the Lord, I've been up all night, praying nonstop! Are you okay? Is Phoebe recovered?" The breathless anxiety in her voice made Jock's chest expand. He could always rely on his mom to love and protect him the only way she knew how. Worry and prayer.

"I'm okay, we're okay, Mom. Phoebe's still in intensive care while they rewarm her. She had some internal bleeding."

Marge gasped. "Oh no. I'll keep praying." She caught her breath. "I'm here with Charlie, at your place. He's slept well, thankfully. The chief came by to check on us. Jake had already relayed what happened. Is it safe to come and see you when Charlie wakes up?"

"I'll check with the nurses. How's the weather out there?" He couldn't see much from his window.

"The storm's gone." She swallowed. "Call me the moment I can bring Charlie, okay?" Was that a sniff? Poor Mom.

"I'm okay, Mom. We're safe." He ended the call then dialed Cal O'Brien. Voicemail. "Hey, O'Brien, give me a call when you can." Then he closed his eyes. May as well rest while he could.

He woke to Chief Anderson standing next to his bed, looking out the window.

Jock cleared his throat. "Chief?"

His boss whirled around, a smile on his face. He took a step toward the bed. "Wow, O'Halloran. That was some scare you gave me."

Great, was he going to get chewed out on top of everything else?

The chief shook his head. "I cannot believe you and Mrs. Tait survived. From what we pieced together from the scene, you shouldn't have. What happened?"

Jock filled him in, starting from when they lost radio contact and ending with the escape from the vehicle.

The chief let out a low whistle. "I'm so proud of you, O'Halloran. Truly."

Normally, the chief's praise would fill Jock with satisfaction. But tonight, the words made him reflect on their meaning. About how close Phoebe had come to death, and how Jock had let it happen. Was that something to be proud of? Not in his book. The recriminations threatened a pile on, but he could let those simmer for later. Now, he needed to concentrate on the debrief.

"The DEA is ecstatic. Between us and the coast guard, we've arrested Caroline and the crew trafficking the latest shipment of fentanyl. The coast guard picked up the crew members from the Bering Sea. Both are exercising their right to remain silent, but I think the DEA will get what they need." The chief sat in the chair. "Your buddy Special Agent O'Brien wasn't best pleased he missed the arrests, but he's on the plane now. Should land this morning." That explained the voicemail.

"Great news, Chief."

"That so? Then why the long face?" The chief raised his eyebrows.

Jock attempted to smile, but it fell flat. "Sorry, Chief, it really is great news. I'm just..." How could he explain?

The chief gave him an appraising look. "You're waiting on news of Mrs. Tait?"

His face slackened. Until he knew for sure she was okay, he could find no satisfaction in the arrests, or anything else.

When he didn't reply, the chief continued, "It's okay to care, Jock."

Regardless of his boss's uncharacteristically soft tone, this wasn't a topic Jock could talk about with him. "Yeah, I guess." He had to change the subject. Fast. "There's one thing I don't understand, though. How did you find us so quickly? Caroline had a heavy-duty signal jammer."

Chief Anderson leaned back and let out a long, slow breath. "Yes, she did. But we caught a break. The DEA got word that a fentanyl shipment would be landing within the next twenty-four hours. They had the US Coast Guard patrolling the shore. The coast guard saw Caroline driving along the road—which seemed a little unusual when anyone in their right mind was off the roads. When they called it into the station, the dispatcher informed them that you were missing. Then Caroline's signal jammer must've run out of juice, because your GPS came back online. Through providence, the fire department were finishing up a call nearby, and I'd come along to assist. All the parts fit together, and we were there in the right place at the right time. Turns out the shipment was headed for Caroline."

Jock's heart filled with humility. The Lord had been working to protect them, answering their prayers. *Lord, forgive me for my doubt.* One name remained. "What about Mason Lane?"

"He's in the wind. The DEA has put out a BOLO, but it's in the US Marshals' hands now. They'll find him." The chief stood. "You look beat. I'll let you get some rest."

At that moment, a doctor in scrubs walked into the room, a smile on his face. A face mask hung from his forearm. "Officer O'Halloran, I have good news."

Jock's heart rose into this throat.

"I'm Dr. Phillips, Mrs. Tait's treating doctor. She asked me to come check on you and let you know she's going to be fine. You did a good job keeping her safe, Officer."

Relief coursed through Jock's limbs, and his shoulders sagged. *It wasn't me, though, Lord. You deserve the praise.*

The chief gave Jock's arm a squeeze and grinned. "I'll leave you to it."

"Her son wants to see her. Is it okay if he comes in for a visit this morning?" Jock bounced a curled knuckle against his mouth.

"Sure, and you can see her now, if you're feeling up to it. Let me get a nurse to help." Dr. Phillips turned and walked through the door.

"I'll call Marge for you." The chief pulled out his phone and walked toward the door.

"Thanks, Chief." Jock swung his legs over the edge of the bed. Surely, he didn't need a nurse to get around. His stomach fluttered with a mix of anticipation and nervousness. Half-finished thoughts of what he should say to Phoebe swirled around his mind, until he resolved to let her do the talking. As he walked to the door, his head spun. *Whoa.* He leaned against the doorframe.

The nurse approached with a wheelchair, giving him a wry grin. "Thought you'd be a tough guy, huh? That blood pressure will sure do it to you. Hop on board. Doctor's orders."

An unpleasant tingling sensation came over the back of his neck as he lowered himself into the chair. "Thanks." He forced a smile, not impressed a nurse could make him feel like he was back in elementary school.

"I'm impressed how well you both recovered." The nurse pushed him down the hall. "We get our fair share of hypothermic patients in here, and not everyone does so well as you. Especially not being in the water that long."

Thank You, Lord. "I'm grateful Mrs. Tait is okay. I was worried about her."

"She's tough. Like you. Obvious she has something to fight for. You can always tell." They paused outside of a room. "Wait here. And by that I mean *wait here*."

Jock gave her a salute, rubbing his hands together. While he might be embarrassed to once again be wheeled in to see Phoebe, he had to swallow his pride. He needed to see she was okay.

The nurse returned. "She's ready for you now."

Jock swallowed then allowed the nurse to wheel him into the room.

Phoebe lay on the bed, her hair splayed out on the pillow. The mattress had been tilted at a thirty degree angle, and she was propped up a little more by pillows. Not quite sitting, but almost. An IV drip had been attached to her along with multiple other wires and monitors. A lump formed in Jock's throat, and he swallowed it down. *I couldn't bear it if anything had happened to her.* Which meant he needed to let her go. No way would he put himself in a position where he might harm Phoebe and Charlie the way Dieter had harmed him and his mom.

Phoebe looked up, her tired eyes bright. "I'm glad you're okay."

Jock smiled, ignoring the weight of longing that filled his chest. "Same here. How are you feeling?"

"Tired." Phoebe pursed her lips. "I don't want to sleep, though, the doctor said Charlie would be here soon." Her eyes shone with unshed tears.

Jock reached for her hand, taking a deep breath. "He's okay. I talked to Mom earlier. They've been staying at my place."

She sniffed. "I was so scared."

Not knowing what to say, Jock ignored the nurse's instructions and rose to sit on the bed. He squeezed her hand. She squeezed back, and his eyes misted. He blinked rapidly, trying to regain control. "I'm sorry."

"For what?" Phoebe sniffed.

"I should've done better. Kept you out of danger." He shook his head.

Phoebe pressed her lips together, and Jock's stomach dropped as he realized Phoebe probably agreed.

But then she slowly shook her head. "You did more than

I could possibly have imagined." Her shoulders drooped. "I don't suppose we will get answers about Ronnie now."

A fluttery feeling entered Jock's chest. It was time to let Phoebe know. "I have information on Ronnie."

FOURTEEN

Phoebe's eyes widened. "What information?" She leaned toward Jock, her heart racing. "Please, just tell me what you know."

Jock maintained eye contact. "My DEA friend, Cal O'Brien, called just before Caroline restrained me. Ronnie's crew was involved in drug trafficking."

"Drugs?" Phoebe's lips parted, and she sifted all the information through this new lens. Could Ronnie have been taking drugs himself? Did that explain his mood swings? His short fuse? She closed her eyes. If he'd been involved in drug trafficking, the stakes were much higher for everyone. *No wonder they needed to cover up his death.*

He swallowed. "We'd suspected it may be something like that, but it was just a theory. It's the only thing that explained why Caroline—or anyone else—would want his death kept quiet. You must've had—must still have—information on their ongoing criminal operation that you don't know about."

"I can't believe it." Phoebe's chest tingled. How could Ronnie have gotten himself into something like that? Had Ethan Davis died because of those drugs? Bile rose in her throat.

Jock clasped his other hand over her wrist. "We'll get

back to the motive, but I'm sorry to say, there's more. The chief came by before and updated me."

"More?" Phoebe's posture slumped as Jock's face became solemn. His expression told her all she needed to know. "Ronnie was definitely murdered, wasn't he?"

"Yes." Jock's expression softened. "I'm so sorry, Phoebe. I know it's not what you wanted to hear."

The pain in his face made her want to comfort him, even though it reflected her own anguish. "Do you know what happened?"

Jock drew a deep breath. "This isn't going to be easy to hear."

"I need to know." A painful tightness formed in Phoebe's throat. She squeezed his hand, thankful he didn't shy away from her emotions.

"Well, your husband did catch fish. He wasn't lying about his profession. Captain Kemp didn't want to attract attention, so they'd go ahead and do their jobs. Only sometimes they'd stray close to a container shipping line. It's not unusual, but there was a pattern—it only happened when ships from specific ports would come by. Each ship has a GPS, so the DEA was able to track that. Anyway, when the right container ship came past, they'd send out a diver—either Ronnie or one of the other crew members—to go dive under it. Packages of fentanyl had been sealed and attached to the bottom of the vessel, ready for the crew to retrieve. The diver would take the package then attach it to the bottom of Kemp's fishing boat. They'd retrieve the drugs when the haul had been inspected and everyone had gone home." He sighed. "All that to say, Ronnie didn't resurface after one of the dives. The DEA suspect Ronnie was blackmailing Caroline, and in retaliation she, or one of the crew, tampered with his oxygen. The crew covered it up."

Phoebe's eyes burned, and she let the tears fall freely. Her husband had been diving for drugs! For fentanyl! Her stomach roiled at the thought of how many lives those drugs had destroyed. Or ended! Ronnie had been a key part of that. *What had he done with the money?* She hadn't seen any unusual transactions. Certainly no payments outside his fishing wages. Did he have another bank account somewhere? Her heart sank. Unless those "fishing wages" were the payments. She'd thought that fishing paid particularly well, and Ronnie had brushed it off as Alaska pay rates. Maybe it didn't. Maybe Ronnie's money had all been drug money. Maybe the house she lived in had been paid for in part through the misery of others. *Now I know.* How could she return to that house knowing that?

She cleared her throat. "I guess it's what I wanted, isn't it?" She blinked back the tears that had started up again. "It's why I came. For answers."

Jock gave a sad smile. "I know it's not what you were expecting. I'm so sorry you've had to go through all this."

Phoebe shook her head. "At least it's over now."

Jock hesitated, his eyes narrowing.

"It *is* over now, isn't it?" Phoebe swallowed, feeling suddenly faint.

"Caroline's accomplice—Mason Lane—is still at large. No one's been able to track him down. The US Marshals Service has fugitive investigators looking for him. He won't get far. But until he's apprehended, it's not over." Jock leaned toward her, stroking her arm. "Until then, I'm not going anywhere."

"I need some space." Phoebe turned away from him, pulling her hand from his. She couldn't deal with anyone right now. The thought of who she'd married. The father of her child. How could she trust anyone ever again?

"Okay." Jock's quiet tone suggested she'd hurt him. Oh, she didn't want to hurt this wonderful man.

"Jock—"

"Mama! Mama!" Charlie burst through the door, his little legs powering toward her.

Phoebe's chest tightened. How would she tell Charlie? This would all come out. His father's name would be searchable online in association with criminals. *Ronnie* was a criminal. She bit the inside of her cheek, willing herself to put on a happy face for her son.

"Charlie!" Hopefully, the child wouldn't notice her sadness.

Jock backed toward the door, slipping out as Beth followed Charlie. He leaned into her ear, saying something Phoebe couldn't make out.

Beth nodded in response, then headed toward Phoebe. She hoisted Charlie onto the bed, where he immediately covered Phoebe's face in kisses.

"I hope you don't mind. Marge was desperate to check in on Jock, so I offered to watch Charlie while you had a visit." She sat in the visitor chair.

Phoebe's heart swelled at Beth's selflessness. "Thank you, Beth. I don't know how I could ever repay you for all you've done."

"You don't need to repay me." Beth smiled. "It's just what we do for each other here. I've had my fair share of help, I can tell you that!" She retrieved Mr. Snuffles, who'd been forgotten on the floor.

"Mama," Charlie crooned, snuggling into Phoebe's chest. Thankfully, the hospital had given her a lot of pain relief, so the action didn't hurt too much.

"He's had a lovely time playing with Marina. They've

really hit it off." Beth rubbed her pregnant belly, wincing. "This little one has a serious kick on him or her."

Phoebe's heart dropped, just a little. "I guess I'll never get to experience that again." She covered her mouth. Where did that come from? She'd typically never say something that personal to someone she knew well, let alone someone she barely knew. *Must be the pain medication.*

"Never say never." Beth smiled, a slight twinkle in her eye.

"No, I won't be remarrying." Phoebe stroked Charlie's head. "I couldn't risk that with him." She blinked rapidly. *Again with the oversharing!*

Beth pursed her lips, a thoughtful expression on her face. "Really? Rachel and I thought we sensed something between you and Jock."

Phoebe's eyes widened. Maybe she hadn't been imagining Jock's feelings.

Beth put her hand to her mouth. "Sorry if that's too personal to say. It's really no one's business."

"It's okay. It just made me think." Phoebe closed her eyes. Maybe it was the painkillers, but could it be she felt a lot less guarded with Beth as well?

"Jock's such a wonderful man. Amazing with kids." Beth giggled. "Sorry, I sound like a matchmaker. I don't mean to. It used to drive me crazy when people would do that to me."

Phoebe smiled. "I don't mind. It's good to hear that. He's been good with Charlie."

"There you go!" Beth clapped her hands.

"Oh. No. No, nothing's going to happen." Phoebe absently stroked Charlie's head, feeling a small measure of contentment. Jock may be good with kids, but now that she knew what Ronnie had done, she had to leave it at that. She had her dance studio back home. That and Charlie would have to be enough.

Her eyes closed as the warm embrace of her son lulled her to sleep. He was counting on her. *I can't let Charlie down.*

Jock's heart felt like lead as he settled into the wheelchair outside Phoebe's room, waiting for the nurse to wheel him back to his room. What a horrible situation he'd created for himself. Why had he allowed himself to fall in love with a woman who'd never feel the same? He lowered his head into his hands. How foolish he'd been to think that Phoebe would open her heart to him. She'd been so clear to his mom that she'd never let a man into her life. And when he thought they had a connection, she'd shut him down. Which had to be for the best. Sons ended up like their fathers. *You'll turn out exactly like Dieter.* No way he'd risk that with Charlie. He cared too much for that.

At least he could take heart in the fact Phoebe and Charlie were safe, and thanks to the arrests, no further harm could come to them. Mason Lane wouldn't have stuck around. Cruz and his colleagues at the USMS would track him down soon.

The blizzard had left as quickly as it had come, and the snowplows were grinding along the streets, clearing away the final drifts of snow. How he wished it could be that easy to clear the baggage from his own life. *Lord, I am trying so hard to follow Your will, but I'm not sure what You want me to do now.*

His mom's voice sounded beside him. "Jock, I've been looking all over for you." The poor woman. She'd probably been terrified the whole night through.

She took him in her arms and hugged him tight. "Boy,

I needed that." She let out a deep sigh, and Jock's heart softened. At least he could always count on his mom to have his back.

She held him at arm's length, inspecting him. She ran her hand over the new bruise on his temple. "She did that, huh?"

Jock nodded, hating the hurt on his mom's face. "I'm sorry about Caroline, Mom. I know she was supposed to be your friend."

Pressing her lips together, she ignored his comment. "I hope you got that checked out. Two concussions…" She clicked her tongue. "Hypothermia. What else?"

"They've taken good care of me. I'm fine. I promise." Jock gave what he hoped was a reassuring smile.

She shook her head. "If you say so. Come on, let's get you back to your room, and you can tell me all about it." She wheeled Jock down the hallway then settled him back into his room. Dipping into her bag, she pulled out a box of homemade chocolate chip cookies.

Jock's mouth watered. "Okay." He sat opposite his mom and took one of the cookies.

"Charlie helped with these ones, that's why there are a few odd shapes." The fondness in his mom's voice made his heart contract a little. They'd both have to give up the fantasy that Phoebe would stay.

"I hope you're making sure Phoebe won't go back to Tucson?" His mom's beady eyes pierced him.

Jock slowly chewed the cookie, buying time. Did she really think he had any control of that? Sometimes he had to wonder. "What do you want me to do?" He raised his eyebrows.

His mom glanced at the ceiling and mouthed, *Give me strength.* "She has a perfectly comfortable home here, including a grandma-on-demand." She glared at him as if willing him to understand.

Jock sighed. "Mom, I know what you're saying, but that's not going to happen."

"Why not?" Her face dropped. "Doesn't Phoebe want to stay?"

"Maybe. But that's not the problem, Mom. *I'm* the problem."

His mom's face wrinkled in confusion. "How?"

"I can't be around her and Charlie. Not with my history." He scrubbed a hand over his face. "And Phoebe knows that. She's just come out of an unhealthy relationship. She's feeling very fragile."

"Your history—" A light of realization appeared on her face. "Oh, no, Jock. Honey, you don't think…" She reached to hold his hand, closing her eyes. "I'm *so* sorry."

"It's not your fault."

She pinched the bridge of her nose, her eyes closed. "You think you're going to be like Dieter, don't you." Wasn't a question. His mom had finally worked it out. "You will *never* be like Dieter. I promise you that."

"You're my mom, you're supposed to say that." Jock rubbed the back of his neck, trying to unclench his jaw.

She squeezed his hand. "I wouldn't lie to you, Jock. Not about something like that." She took her hand back and grabbed a cookie of her own, taking a thoughtful nibble.

Jock waited for her to speak, reaching for another cookie then putting it down again. His appetite had left him.

"Dieter was a prideful, self-obsessed man-child. He treated you badly because you frustrated him. It wasn't your fault—young children can be very frustrating." She gave him a pointed look. "But instead of being the adult he was supposed to be and exercising an ounce of self-control, he threw tantrums. The man was incapable of putting the needs of others above his own." She raised her eyebrows. "Does that sound like you?"

He opened his mouth to reply, but she held up her hand.

"That was a rhetorical question, Jock. You *know* that's not like you at all. No one could do your job without the kind of sacrificial love for neighbor Dieter couldn't even dream about. That's a fact. Let alone all the other reasons and personality traits I could mention. You're your *father's* son, not your stepfather's."

A pain rose in Jock's throat. "Even if that's true, it doesn't matter. Phoebe isn't interested in any man. Not after her first husband."

His mom shook her head. "I thought I raised you better than that."

"What do you mean by that?" Jock's jaw stiffened.

"I'm not saying you have to marry the woman tomorrow! But don't be a fool and write off the connection you two have just because she's cautious. Anyone with eyes can see the way she looks at you. Phoebe needs people around her who love her, and you are quite obviously someone who loves her." Marge crossed her arms in front of her chest and leaned back. "Pluck up your courage and tell her!"

A light flutter of hope in Jock's stomach caused his shoulders to relax. Maybe his mom had a point. She'd been through a lot in her life and knew more than most about relationships. And though he'd never admit it, she probably knew him better than anyone.

The theory all sounded great coming from his mom's mouth, but could it really be that easy? He let out a long, slow breath. None of it mattered unless he could convince Phoebe. *Lord, please give me the words I need.*

FIFTEEN

It was late afternoon when a soft tap on the door preceded Jock's arrival. Phoebe's heart leaped for a moment before coming back down to earth with a thud. *There's no hope there.* She had to get her head back to the reality of her life. After being spoiled by the nurses, Charlie had fallen asleep next to her. Beth had left, promising that Marge would come by and get the boy later. Charlie's soft snuffles reminded her that she must guard her heart. For him.

Jock wore his uniform, and he was clean-shaven. "I've been discharged." He lowered himself into the seat next to the bed.

"Did someone launder your uniform?"

"No, this is a spare I had in my locker. Miller dropped it by." He shucked his jacket, hanging it over the arm of the chair. "How's Charlie doing?" He peeked at the little boy, a slight smile on his face.

Phoebe stroked her son's head. "He's fine. As much as he loves Marge and Beth, he needs his mom." She swallowed. "Thanks again for making sure I could be here. I cannot imagine how hard it would've been for him if I'd died."

"Don't even think about that." Jock ran his hands down his thighs. "When do the doctors think you'll be ready to leave hospital?" He pressed his hands between his knees. Could he be nervous?

"It depends how I do in the next twenty-four hours. I'm feeling okay, but they keep saying something about my blood pressure." Phoebe shrugged. "I guess with the case wrapping up, I need to think about booking plane tickets."

"About that..." Jock cleared his throat.

The sincerity in his eyes sent a wave of uncertainty through her heart. *What am I doing?* Holding out hope? For what? Disappointment?

"I've been thinking..." The heartfelt tone of those words made Phoebe's stomach flutter with longing.

The door flung open, and a man stepped into the room.

Jock stood, turning to face him. "This is a private room." His voice held the authority of an officer of the law, with no trace of his earlier softness.

The man's eyes narrowed, and he drew a gun, pointing it at Jock's head. "Get out of the way. This doesn't concern you."

Phoebe reflexively pressed the buzzer next to her then reached for Charlie. Her body screamed in pain as she bent toward him, and she gasped. The pain relief must be wearing off.

Jock stood his ground. "Mason Lane."

Lane growled. "Step aside and give me the kid, or I'll put a bullet through you."

A nurse appeared behind him, took one look at the gun and raced down the hall. Had the man seen her? *Lord, please don't let this man hurt anyone.*

"No. You won't make it past the front door. Put the weapon down. Now!" The aggression in Jock's voice had jarred Phoebe earlier. It didn't this time. He was protecting her and Charlie. *Lord, please protect him.*

"I just need the kid!" the man growled.

"Drop the gun!" Jock stepped forward, his hands up like he was getting ready to grab the man.

The PA system announced a code silver, and Mason Lane stepped forward. "Have it your way." The man fired, and Jock stumbled back a few steps with a grunt.

"No." Jock forced the words out, lunging for Lane and tackling him to the ground. The gun clattered to the floor, and Jock wrestled his assailant.

Charlie started to cry, and Phoebe fought through the pain, grabbing him and pulling him to her as she slipped off the bed and crouched behind it. The IV cannula yanked painfully from her hand, and she pressed the wound to stop the blood flow. Why did the man want Charlie? It didn't make sense. Caroline had been arrested. Why wasn't he on the road, running from the law?

She peered over to see Lane punch Jock in the head. Jock slumped to the ground, and Phoebe stifled a scream. There was nothing to stop the attacker from grabbing the gun and finishing Charlie off! She clutched her son to herself. *Lord, where are You? I need Your—*

Before she could finish her prayer, two hospital security guards rushed through the door. They dragged Mason Lane off Jock. Phoebe strained to see. Lane tried to throw the men off him, but they had him gripped tight. Her attention returned to Jock. He remained still. *Why isn't he moving?* Time slowed. A prickling dread welled up inside her chest as she fixed her gaze on the man who'd demonstrated time and time again that he could be trusted. That he wasn't like Ronnie. Or his stepfather. And maybe, just maybe, he'd been trying to tell her how he felt when they were in the ocean. When he'd kissed her cheek like it might be the last thing they did on this earth. *Oh no!*

Charlie wailed in her arms, his sobs breaking her heart. She held him close. "Shhh, it's okay. They've caught the bad man." What else could she say?

"Juh!" Charlie cried. "Juh!"

Phoebe's body felt hollowed out. Charlie cared for Jock. Her two-year-old son understood that Jock needed help. Where were the doctors and nurses? Why weren't they doing something? The security guards had restrained Mason Lane and were in the process of cuffing him.

No one was coming. "Charlie, we need to help Jock." She scooped Charlie up with her, breathing through the pain that radiated through her body like an explosion.

She hustled around the bed then kneeled next to Jock's unconscious body.

Mason Lane grumbled and writhed as the security guards pulled him from the room, but Phoebe ignored him. She had to help Jock.

"Jock!" Phoebe cried. "Wake up! Please!"

"Juh!" Charlie joined in the cry, clutching her with one hand. Mr. Snuffles dropped to the floor as he patted Jock with the other.

Jock didn't move. Phoebe stroked his cheek, her tears dropping to his face. "Please, Jock. You have to wake up. You've survived everything else. Come on!" She sobbed. "Jock, I love you!"

Jock's eyes fluttered.

"Please, Lord." Phoebe's breath shuddered.

"We've got it from here." The gentle voice of a doctor interrupted. His hand rested on her shoulder.

Phoebe looked up. Two nurses accompanied him. She grabbed Charlie, scooping up Mr. Snuffles as she backed away to let them do their job. Charlie protested, reaching for Jock.

"It's okay. He'll be okay," she soothed. *Lord, please let him be okay.*

Phoebe sank into the chair near the bed while the doctors worked on him. She caught snatches of their conversation. Low heart rate. Light sensitivity.

She stared at him, willing him to come to. None of her previous concerns mattered now. Not Ronnie's behavior. Not her own fears about her judgment. She yearned to move on from the pain, the recriminations and the lies she'd experienced in her life. She'd witnessed the Lord come and rescue her in her despair. He'd used this wonderful man to do it. *You sent him to me, didn't You, Lord?* An orderly raced in with a backboard.

Phoebe couldn't stay and watch. She bundled Charlie into her arms, carrying him past Jock and through the door while the adrenaline allowed. She settled onto one of the visitor chairs, letting Charlie slip to the floor to play with Mr. Snuffles. She bowed her head. *Lord, please heal him. Help him to recover. I need him.* A sense of peace came over her. She knew then Jock would be okay. *Thank You.*

Jock proved he wouldn't hurt her. He'd risked his life time and again for her. He'd taken a bullet to save her son. His own fears of turning out like his stepfather were completely unfounded. In the short time she'd come to know him, he'd shown her more of himself than Ronnie had ever shown. He'd proved his generosity, his patience, his courage and so much more. But could he take a leap of faith with her and Charlie?

Jock felt disoriented and groggy. Couldn't open his eyes. But he remembered something. Phoebe's voice, telling him she loved him. *I wasn't hallucinating that, was I, Lord?*

He couldn't have been. Those words had spurred him on. Forced his body to keep going. To heal.

"He's coming around." An unfamiliar male voice spoke close to him.

Jock forced his eyes open, blinking in the light.

"Welcome back, Officer. Do you know where you are?" The man wore a white coat, and a stethoscope hung around his neck.

"Hospital." Jock's voice sounded foreign to him.

"That's right. You weren't out for long, but we're going to take you for a CT scan now you're awake." The doctor stepped back and allowed one of the orderlies to prepare the bed to be wheeled.

They pushed the bed down the corridor, past the visitor area.

"Juh!" Charlie's voice sent a wash of love through Jock's heart. He'd put himself in the line of fire. Dieter never would've done that. The lingering fears and lies that he'd been telling himself for so long slipped away. All the truth his mom, Samuel and others had told him became real. *I'm not my stepfather. I'm no danger to Charlie or Phoebe.*

"Jock, you're awake." Phoebe's breathless voice came close, and he turned his head.

"We're just taking him for a scan. You can see him when he gets back." The doctor held out his hand to stop Phoebe from approaching.

"No." Jock found his voice. "This can't wait." No way would he let this chance slip through his fingers. He had Phoebe here, now. If he'd learned anything in the past week, it was to not delay.

"Five minutes." The doctor stepped back to let Phoebe through.

Phoebe hoisted Charlie on her hip. "Your mom's on the

way. I'll call her, let her know you're awake." Tears glinted in her eyes.

He reached for her hand, and she gripped it like a lifeline. "Phoebe, I love you. I don't want you to go home. I'm sorry I didn't say it before. I want to be a husband to you, and a dad to Charlie."

Phoebe's eyes darted between him and the doctor, and Jock almost smiled.

"I'm not saying this because of a head injury. I promise. I love you, Phoebe, and I heard you say you loved me. That wasn't a hallucination, was it?" A lump formed in Jock's throat.

"No, it wasn't." Tears released down Phoebe's cheeks, and she looked around before handing Charlie to a nurse. "I love you, Jock O'Halloran, and I want to be your wife." She bent down, taking his face in her hands and kissing him.

Jock's heart expanded as the woman he loved stroked his face, releasing him from the kiss.

Charlie giggled and made happy kissing noises. "Juh!"

Phoebe pulled away from him, keeping hold of his hand. "That's right, Charlie. It's Jock. You want to stick around here in Alaska?" Her eyes shone as she met Jock's gaze again.

"Yah!" The toddler held his arms out toward his mom, and a gentle warmth came over Jock. Their little family would be okay. Better than okay. He'd make sure of it.

EPILOGUE

One month later...

Phoebe stood on the threshold of her home in Tucson, her key hovering near the lock. Her arm had just come out of the cast, and the diamond solitaire on her ring finger glittered in the sun.

"Are you sure you want to do this?" Jock placed his hand on her back, stroking her with his thumb. "We can still get someone else to come and sort through it all."

"I'm sure." Phoebe swallowed. She needed to go through the house herself. It would go on the market soon, and stagers would come in to make it look beautiful. But she wanted to put her and Charlie's past to rest. She turned the key in the lock. "Let's start in the garage and work from there."

Half an hour later, Jock had sorted through Ronnie's tools, and Phoebe had classified most of the gardening equipment. They'd donate them all to the local church, except for a few things for Charlie—Jock had convinced her that Charlie would need a handful of mementos from his dad.

Phoebe trusted his judgment. He and Charlie had bonded quickly. The little boy sought him out often, calling him

Juh. Seemed to Phoebe that any fear Jock may have had about not bonding with Charlie was gone. He couldn't be a more loving and protective stepfather if he tried. During those quiet times when she thought about all Jock had lost when his own father had died, her heart ached for him.

"What do you want to do with this?" Jock caught her attention, holding the mid-nineteenth-century painting of the Philadelphia Navy Yard.

Phoebe bit her lip. "I don't know if you'd consider it an heirloom. What do you think?"

Jock turned the painting over. "Huh. Looks like it's had a false back put on it." He carefully peeled away the cardboard, and his eyes widened.

"What've you found?" Phoebe dropped the gloves she'd been holding and walked over.

He shook his head incredulously. "I think I've just discovered Ronnie's blackmail stash. Look at this." He held up a handwritten ledger. "Each of the shipments. Dates, times, the names of the container ship. Number of packages. Everything."

Phoebe's stomach dropped. "No wonder Caroline didn't want me to survive. She knew I'd find this eventually. It'd be the end for her." In exchange for a deal with the US attorney, Mason Lane had told them everything. Caroline had paid him to snatch Charlie, and he'd diligently continued on his mission because he wanted the final payment. He didn't realize she'd already been arrested. Phoebe shuddered at the memory.

Jock took her in his arms. "It's over now. Caroline is already going to prison for the rest of her life. Now the DEA has the evidence to go after everyone else involved." He put the painting aside. "You don't have to worry about a thing, thanks to the Lord." How thankful she was that the Lord had protected them.

"Mmm." Phoebe closed her eyes, sinking into Jock as he kissed her.

Jock pulled back, stroking her face. "I'd better take some photos to send to O'Brien. We'll bring the original with us."

"Good idea." Phoebe went back to her work, finishing off the garage before heading to the laundry.

She folded a spare toddler sleeping bag that she'd hung on a rack to dry before she left for Cordova. How thankful she was for her new friends Rachel and Beth. They'd supported and encouraged her to remain in Cordova, gathering together enough supplies for her and Charlie that they didn't want for anything. The women had scouted out a vacant tenancy for her dance studio, and gauged interest for the classes throughout the local school and beyond. To Phoebe's surprise, the community desperately wanted a dance studio—a few children were even keen on flying in from smaller towns.

While they were here in Tucson, she'd go by her old studio and finalize the paperwork assigning her share to Keziah. Her old friend had put aside her disappointment and supported her wholeheartedly. Phoebe planned to catch up with her mom. Thanks to her renewed relationship with the Lord, Phoebe had put aside all the animosity she'd harbored toward her mom and accepted her as she was. Modifying her expectations had helped. Her mom was never going to be like Marge, and that was okay.

By the time Phoebe had loaded the cleaning supplies into boxes, Jock was done in the garage. He held a small box he'd labelled *Charlie*. "This warmer weather here is making me think about my training. I wonder if I'll have passed before summer. I'd like to get a puppy while it's warmer."

Phoebe smiled. "How do you think Bruce will feel, having another K-9 around?"

"He'll be pleased to have some company. Besides, when have I ever run out of treats?" Jock laughed.

"True." Phoebe's heart glowed for her fiancé. When Chief Anderson agreed to Jock undertaking K-9 training, Jock had been beside himself with joy. Hadn't hurt that the chief had been so grateful his officer had recovered that he'd have said yes to just about anything.

"Come on, let's start on the bathroom. Then we can have lunch." Jock guided Phoebe down the hall.

The thought of a simple lunch together misted Phoebe's eyes. Never could she have imagined that she'd have this in her life. A mother-in-law who loved Charlie like he was her own grandson. A fiancé who'd go to the ends of the earth for her.

Now both of them were on the precipice of doing what they loved, in a place they loved. Most importantly, they had each other. *Lord, thank You.*

* * * * *

Dear Reader,

Thank you for reading *Alaskan Abduction Target*. I hope that you loved Jock and Phoebe getting their well-deserved happily-ever-after as much as I did! I hope you also took comfort in Phoebe's journey back to our Lord and Savior Jesus Christ. I have such compassion for Phoebe. How many times have we felt like we're failing in our walk with our Lord? We all stumble, perhaps wondering whether He still accepts us. But as Phoebe learned, our Lord is the Good Shepherd. For those of us who have repented and responded to His call, there is nothing that can separate us from His love. As far as we stray from Him, He will always come and guide us back to green pastures, with rejoicing! We only have to ask.

Blessings,
Megan

PS. You can find more of my books and writing via www.meganshort.net